No Plac

After a hard day on the job, Harry Tasker looked forward to going home. It was tough work crashing a fortress-mansion in the Swiss alps . . . breaking into the super-computer of a money master who spread tentacles of evil around the globe . . . trying to resist going to bed with a dazzling beauty who clearly was ready, willing and able . . . and escaping in the glow of an explosion and a hail of bullets.

But now Harry was heading home to his loving wife, who thought he was a decent if rather boring computer salesman . . . to his daughter, who worshipped him as her big, kindly bear of a dad . . . to the peace and quiet he craved after his job as Operative 0024 for the U.S. Omega Agency.

Harry didn't know it, but a new front was about to open up in his war against terror and for survival.

The most dangerous front of all.

The home front.

True Lies

True Lies

A NOVEL BY

Dewey Gram and Duane Dell 'Amico

FROM THE SCREENPLAY BY

James Cameron

A SIGNET BOOK

SIGNET

Published by the Penguin Group
Penguin Books Ltd, 27 Wrights Lane, London W8 5TZ, England
Penguin Books USA Inc., 375 Hudson Street, New York, New York 10014, USA
Penguin Books Australia Ltd, Ringwood, Victoria, Australia
Penguin Books Canada Ltd, 10 Alcorn Avenue, Toronto, Ontario, Canada M4V 3B2
Penguin Books (NZ) Ltd, 182–190 Wairau Road, Auckland 10, New Zealand

Penguin Books Ltd, Registered Offices: Harmondsworth, Middlesex, England

First published in the USA by Signet, an imprint of Dutton Signet,
a division of Penguin Books USA Inc., 1994
First published in Great Britain by Signet 1994
1 3 5 7 9 10 8 6 4 2

One

All Harry Tasker could think about was his balls. Two dozen armed guards, floodlights, vicious Dobermans, and a state-of-the-art security system awaited him only eight feet away. But Harry had more pressing problems. His *cojones* were trying to migrate back up into his body. They had painfully squeezed themselves into a space the size and appearance of a big walnut. And that was because Harry floated eight feet under an ice-covered lake, cutting the metal bars that shut him out of Jamal Khaled's fortress chateau high in the Swiss Alps.

On the bright side, his oxygen-arc cutting tool was beginning to create warm convection currents. He kicked his jet-fins, moving his frozen maracas closer to the heat. He grinned around his regulator. Aaaah. One bar came away and drifted gently to the bottom.

The Alpine peaks were breathtaking in the light of a full moon; hard shadows accentuated their chiseled angularity, and glittering blankets of snow, chill and silent as the night sky, fanned down from them. The snow surrounded and gently penetrated the forested saddle in which Khaled's chateau nestled.

There was a party tonight, and the guards hated parties. They were trained to kill anyone trying to get in. But tonight they had to watch helplessly as dozens of cars poured into the motor court, and guests strolled casually, laughing even, through the chateau's massive front doors.

It made the guards nervous, and that made them mad. Their xenon searchlights swept the approaches with more than usual thoroughness; and if they blinded a few limo drivers, so what. They eyed the arriving guests with disconcerting coldness, and only halfheartedly rebuked the attack dogs when they barked and bared fangs at fur-coated men and diamond-encrusted women.

The guests felt the chill, and were glad to get inside to the relative warmth of the head butler. He greeted them each courteously, discreetly passed their watermarked invitations under an ultraviolet light, then took their coats and handed them off to white-gloved security personnel, who politely but thoroughly searched them with hand-held metal detectors.

Meanwhile on the east wall, a lone guard, warm and watchful inside his white exposure suit, scanned the icy lake. The lake approach was completely exposed, and the ice treacherously thin, but his platoon leader had mercilessly drilled every ounce of complacency out of his body. He knew that his beat passed over one of the few sizable breaks in the ramparts other than the main gate: the boat canal that connected Khaled's private docks with the lake outside. It was a part of his beat he checked carefully and often. He went there now.

A heavy grating of steel bars closed off the canal entrance, locked down by thin blue ice. The bars, as the guard knew, ran all the way to the bottom. He scanned the ice and grating carefully.

Most other nights he would have immediately unslung his FN FAL rifle and barked an alert into his walkie-talkie, an alert that would have resulted in Harry Tasker looking like Switzerland's most famous cheese. But tonight there was just enough ambient moonlight, and just enough snow on the translucent ice to block out the dim glow of Harry's torch.

The guard looked out over the lake and moved on.

Harry turned off his torch and let it fall. A hole in the grating big enough for a large man—which is what Harry was—opened into the darkness of the canal.

Harry pulled himself through. His powerful legs scissored, propelling him rapidly forward.

A bright-eyed Doberman rounded the corner of Khaled's boathouse, leading his master on the end of a choker chain. The guard looked out over the floodlit dock that jutted into the canal. All clear; all quiet. They walked away, and as the dull thud of the guard's boots faded, a faint chipping sound issued from the shadows under the dock.

A piece of ice broke quietly free, lifted upward an inch or two and slid back. Then another. Harry Tasker's hooded head slowly lifted from the dark

water and looked around in every direction. He
slipped his regulator and goggles off and smiled. He
was inside.

Harry unslung a waterproof pack, and then his
tank, which he let drop. Then he froze, silent as a
water snake, with only his eyes showing above the
surface. Another guard walked by at the edge of
the canal.

The guard's eyes swept the dock, but did not
penetrate the shadows beneath. He walked on,
around the boathouse and out of sight.

Harry kicked off his fins, took a final look around,
and swiftly pulled himself up a frozen ladder onto
the dock. He moved like a ninja into the shadows of
the boathouse.

Opening his pack, he pulled out a walkie-talkie
and thumbed the transmit button.

"Honey, I'm home," he said.

"Roger that," said Gib.

Albert "Gib" Gibson was a real mensch. Unless you
were a nuclear terrorist, or one of his ex-wives. A
twenty-year man with the Omega Sector, his total
dedication to the agency's mission was now chipping
away at his third marriage. Both the terrorists and
his spouses wished he'd spend more time at home.

Gib didn't look much like the super spies in mov-
ies, and certainly didn't act like one, but he had been
Harry Tasker's mission coordinator and closest friend
for over a decade. Harry owed Gib his life many
times over. Harry knew that a couple of inches
behind Gib's comfortable beer gut was a rock-hard
wall of muscle; and that behind the puckish face and

irreverent humor was the iciest and fastest thinking mind in Omega Sector.

Just then, Gib sat hunched in a surveillance van parked on a winding mountain road a half mile away and overlooking the floodlit chateau. Putting a hand over his headset's microphone, he called out the open door of the van.

"Hey, Fize! Get your butt in here. Harry's inside."

Fast Faisil, cyberjock extraordinaire, stood outside carefully peeing his sweetheart's name into a snowbank. Ever security conscious, he was disguising his handwriting by using his left hand. He was twenty-five, Iranian-American, and the most talented hacker Omega Sector ever recruited. Harry always demanded, and got, the best.

Finishing his sentimental homage, Faisil zipped up and jumped back in the van. Placing his eye against the eyepiece of a huge telephoto nightvision scope, he scanned the grounds of the chateau, the eerie green image coming to rest on Khaled's boathouse.

Concealed in the shadows of the boathouse, Harry tore off his neoprene hood and shucked his drysuit. Underneath, he wore black tux pants, a silk cummerbund and bowtie, and a formal shirt with pearl studs. The frogman had suddenly turned into a handsome playboy prince.

From his waterproof bag, he pulled a tiny plug, like a hearing aid, and shoved it deep in his ear canal: a subvocal transceiver. Harry had only to mumble quietly and the transceiver picked up his words from the vibrations inside his head. And not even a dance partner could hear the incoming.

"Switching to subvocal," Harry said quietly. "Gib, you copy?"

The answer came back: "It's Talkradio. You're on the air."

Harry slipped into his shoulder harness—his .45 auto Glock-22 holstered on one side, a transmitter pack for the earpiece slung on the other. He pulled a formal dinner jacket from the pack and slipped it on, concealing the rig.

Then a final touch. He reached in the bag and withdrew a tiny vial of cologne. Harry usually wore a scent with a citrus or sandalwood base—Armani or Atkinson's. But in cold weather he knew a musky vanilla base played better with the ladies, adding back that intimate languor, the sensuality and warmth that the chill sucked away. Tonight the label on the vial read "Obsession."

Harry slapped some on his big square jaw, ran his hands through his hair, straightened his tie, then strode confidently into the floodlights, crossing quickly to the rear of the main house.

With each step, his mind lit brighter; his body warmed and loosened, letting its power flow. Genetics, a fierce will, and endless training had made Harry's body something extraordinary. He just *did* it. Things that no one else could do. Neither his body nor his mind had ever failed him. And so as he walked forward into the middle of Khaled's lethal security apparatus, he found himself grinning like an animal.

It was party time.

Harry walked into the crowded kitchen like he owned it. The cooks and waiters scurried out of his way, too busy to notice or care who he was. He was a ship, and they the water sliding off his bow. Harry finger-tasted a dish as he sailed through, admonishing an assistant chef in excellent French: "This needs more garlic." He pushed through the right-hand swinging door and entered the main room.

The party was in full swing. Harry blended smoothly into the crowd. Foreign dignitaries, businessmen, and minor Mideast nobility mingled with stodgy bankers and playboy arms dealers attended by entire harems. He could smell the high-octane mixture of new oil money and old European wealth.

Harry strolled amiably among the glittering women and cigar-smoking men, casually snagging a glass of champagne and a canapé from the ubiquitous waiters. He nodded to people like he knew them, even greeted a passing sheik in fluent Arabic.

People in his wake looked at each other with raised eyebrows. "Do we know him?" Then they shrugged and went on with their conversations. If they couldn't place him, he couldn't be important.

So Harry glided on through the crowd, scanning over heads. He was looking for someone special, and soon he spotted him.

"Thar she blows. Daddy Petrobucks," he mumbled to Gib.

In the center of the room, fat, manic Jamel Khaled greeted his guests, chattering like a bird and popping canapés from a tray held by a long-suffering waiter anchored at his right hand.

"Thank God I'm rich! Life's too short to stuff a mushroom!" crowed Khaled. He laughed delightedly at his own wit, his plump red lips shining with grease. Everyone around him laughed, too, because a rich man's joke is always funny.

Harry moved on, smiling sweetly at a banker's wife, planning to keep a watch on Khaled out of the corner of his eye. But that was not to be, for a woman walked up to the fat man and greeted him, and Harry found his head turning as if against his will.

She was breathtakingly beautiful, somehow managing to be both lithe and voluptuous at the same time. Something Khaled said made her throw back her head and laugh, and it was the rich, full-chested laugh of an unfettered spirit. Harry's heart began beating faster than it had all night. The woman tossed her black hair and leaned close to Khaled's ear. She and Khaled excused themselves and walked off, absorbed in serious conversation. Harry moved closer, curious now, continuing to stare at her.

It was then that the woman glanced up, catching his eyes. Harry smiled. Her frank gaze held steady a moment, returning his interest, and then his smile. Then the crowd shifted, cutting off their view of each other.

"Mmmmm," said Harry.

"Harry," came the voice in his ear, "You dog. Are you getting a blow job? Nuclear terrorists, remember?"

"Woof. You shoulda seen the warheads on this babe. I'm heading upstairs."

Harry mounted the grand staircase to the second floor, then meandered through a sprinkling of guests admiring a collection of antiquities on the second-floor balcony. Harry glanced around, making sure he was unobserved. He slipped through a door into the corridor of the mansion's private west wing.

Jamel Khaled's library was empty, dark, but not silent. A lock pick was clicking and clacking around in the keyhole of the door. With a final satisfying click, the door swung open and Harry entered, quickly and silently closing it behind him. He walked over to the French windows, opened one, and walked onto the terrace. Above him, a third-floor balcony jutted from the chateau's wall.

Harry leapt onto the rail at the side of the terrace and climbed up the outside wall of the chateau. Iron fingers hooked the masonry's deep bed joints. Feet pushed off against a second-floor cornice. Harry vaulted over the balcony's balustrade and landed in a soft crouch.

Out came the slide pick, and seconds later Harry stepped through another French window into Jamel Khaled's private study.

"I'm in Porky's office."

"Go for it, buddy."

Beautiful antiques and priceless paintings glinted in the moonlight slanting through the windows. Etruscan vases, Greek busts, a Vermeer, a van Gogh still life. Harry didn't give a shit. He went straight to the giant desk and sat down at the computer, booting it up. The hard disk and fan whined up to speed as Harry pulled a flat box the size of a paperback from his jacket pocket and connected it to the modem port.

"Modem in place. Transmitting . . . now."

Harry pushed a button and a green light on the modem began its intelligent blinking as it sucked out Khaled's data and pumped it away.

* * *

In the van, Gib watched eagerly as Faisil punched keys with blurring speed. A monitor scrolled rapidly, crammed from edge to edge with characters.

Faisil spoke into his own headset: "Affirmatory. We are in."

Faisil's fingers never seemed to pause. The data shifted and lurched, reconfiguring inside a familiar Windows environment. A password dialogue box superimposed itself.

"These files are iced *and* encrypted, guys." Faisil *liked* that. "This is going to take me a few minutes."

Gib got on the line with Harry: "Faisil's the man now, buddy. Get your tail out of there."

Getting out of the chateau without alerting the guards was as important as getting in unobserved. So after climbing back down to the library, Harry was extra careful cracking the door into the hall, and very slow sticking out his tiny mirror. He tilted it this way and that, flipped it over, looked the other way, then stepped into the hallway and closed the door quietly behind him. He strode off down the hall, breathing a small sigh of relief—just as a guard rounded the corner ten feet away.

Harry stopped in his tracks, grinned sheepishly, and held out his hands in the universal gesture of "Where the hell am I?"

"Where's the john around here?" said Harry in Arabic. "I have to take a major leak."

The guard hesitated, then warily pointed down the corridor, back toward the party.

"Thanks." Harry nodded. He hurried by, moaning in mock discomfort.

Harry sauntered down the grand staircase and

rejoined the glittering crowd in the main room. Again he grabbed a flute of champagne, affecting polite ennui as he scanned the room. Two security guards were moving toward him, speaking into walkies, heading for the stairs. Harry turned away, suddenly fascinated by a large fragment of bas-relief mounted on a nearby wall. It was a temple frieze depicting four horses drawing a war chariot. Harry found himself wishing he was in the van.

Someone walked up beside him, bringing along the scent of musk. Harry turned and found himself staring into the most beautiful eyes he had ever seen. It was the woman with the multimegaton payload.

"Magnificent, aren't they," he said, slowly turning to indicate the figures on the wall.

"Yes. They are," she said and her voice was like smoke from dry ice. She bathed Harry in an apprais- ing stare. "I'm Juno Skinner. I thought I knew most of Khaled's friends but I don't believe I know you."

Harry offered her his hand. "Renquist," he said. "Harry Renquist." And he smiled delightedly, as he always did when he lied.

In the surveillance van, Gib had heard it all and initiated a global search of the mission database. "Skinner. Skinner. Come on . . ." Juno's picture and data file appeared on his screen. Gib read it out loud: "Juno Skinner. Art and antiquities dealer, specializing in ancient Persia."

Back at the party, Harry tore his eyes away from Juno's bewitching face and turned to the frieze.

"This is Persian if I'm not mistaken."

"Very good. It's sixth century B.C. Do you like the period?"

Harry grinned shamelessly. "I adore it."

* * *

Faisil was still lost in cyberspace, hacking at the ice
surrounding Khaled's data; so it was Gib who pressed
his eye into the starlight scope and saw what they all
wanted least to see. One of the chateau's guards was
leaning over the edge of the dock, shining a flashlight
on the hole in the ice, and then on the trail of
footprints leading away. The guard lifted his head
and called out. A second guard ran over as the first
barked something urgent into his walkie.

Gib pulled up his headset mike. "Harry, we got a
problem. Guards are swarming all over the dock."

Harry was watching Juno over the lip of his champagne flute when he got the message. He turned
toward the stairs and saw Khaled's security chief
listening to his walkie-talkie. The chief barked orders into the walkie, then gestured to three of his
men. They moved swiftly down the stairs, scanning
the crowd.

Harry turned smoothly away and took Juno's arm.
"Do you dance, Ms. Skinner?" Juno smiled. "De-
lighted." They put down their glasses and walked
arm in arm toward the dance floor.

Gib managed to roll his eyes while peering into the
nightvision scope. Harry had stirred up a hornet's
nest. Guards ran across the grounds of the chateau,
unslinging rifles, jabbering into walkies.

Gib looked up from the scope, giving Faisil a
pleading look. "Fize, you've got seconds."

Faisil smiled, though his fingers never slowed.
"Files are unlocked. I'm in. I'm down baby. I got my
hand up her dress and I'm going for the gold. I'm—"

"Just copy the goddam files!" Gib pulled up his

headset mike. "Harry, don't be stopping to smell the roses, now. You hear me, Harry?"

Harry whirled Juno aggressively across the dance floor. She responded deftly, parrying each of his moves with a flourish, showing both grace and hidden power. They were a perfect temperamental match. A kind of surprised reappraisal flashed through both their minds. A worthy and lovely woman, thought Harry. And *hot*. He leaned her down in an Astaire move and swept her back up. She twirled into the crook of his arm and the music ended.

Their eyes were inches apart, their faces glowing with a lusty flush. Wow, was the thought that passed through both their minds. They separated, their hands letting go reluctantly. Juno gave him a wry grin.

"*Well*. And I thought this was going to be just another bunch of boring bankers and oil billionaires."

"Harry," came the voice over the subvocal, "Seconds count. Ditch the bitch, let's go."

"Unfortunately, Juno," Harry said sincerely, "I have a plane to catch."

Juno slipped a card out of some invisible pocket in her sheer dress and handed it to Harry, her eyes locked with his. "Call me if you'd like to see some of my other pieces."

"I'd like that," Harry said.

Faisil still jacked in and hacking, had heard everything over his headset. "Schweeng," he said.

Gib just gaped in disbelief, handed over his mike. "Son of a bitch is with her two minutes and she's ready to bear his children." He took his hand away. "What's your exit strategy, Twinkle Toes?"

"I'm going to walk out the front door," returned Harry.

Gib blinked. "Ballsy . . . Stupid, but ballsy."

And that's what Harry did. He strode out the front door of the chateau, nodding absently to the security men, and clipping down the steps to the broad terrace above the motor court.

Behind Harry, a guard lowered his walkie-talkie and started after him, calling out: "May I see your invitation, sir?"

Without turning, Harry slipped a small flat box out of his breast pocket. It had only one distinguishing feature: a button.

"Here's my invitation," said Harry. And he pressed the button.

Kaboom. Khaled's third-floor office windows blew out in a roiling fireball. The price for a still life by van Gogh went up another notch.

And though the guard had looked toward the explosion for only a split second, when he turned again, Harry was gone.

Half a mile away, Gib started the van, watching the rising fireball. "Aw, shit. Here we go." He stomped on it, fishtailing onto the road, heading downhill.

Meanwhile, Harry sprinted across Khaled's snow-covered lawn, discovering that extra little bit of speed that seems to materialize when you're being fired at with automatic weapons. He flew into a stand of trees, the snow around him exploding with bullet hits, trees splintering into toothpicks. Harry whirled and raised his Glock. *Blam Blam.* Two sprinting guards suddenly jumped backward, kicked in the chest by Harry's hollow points. *Blam Blam*. Another snow angel. *Blam Blam Blam* and a guard in a snowmobile noticed he was sitting in the snow, and there was this Bright Light, and his mommy was reaching out to him . . . .

Harry was high-stepping toward Khaled's wall. Two hungry Dobermans pelted toward him, leaping gracefully in perfect unison. Harry caught them in midleap and knocked their heads together with a crack like a baseball bat. The dogs yelped and dropped to the ground, wobbling like drunks.

"Stay!" said Harry, and sprinted on. Another Doberman lunged out of the nowhere and leapt for his throat. Never breaking stride, Harry caught the dog with one big hand and shot-putted it into a tree. Dog Fu. The dog yelped and whined, scrambling desperately to hold onto the icy branch, its eyes wide in canine amazement.

Harry saw his goal straight ahead—a ten-foot rampart. He hit it at a dead run. His foot hit about three feet up and catapulted him skyward. He grabbed the lip of the wall and vaulted over, dropping into a snowbank and surfing it downhill. He hit the slope standing up and sprinted down the slop, heading for the trees and the highway beyond. A glance back at a guard station revealed the next obstacle.

Two guards on skis emerged from a guardhouse, pumping their ski poles, quickly picking up speed. Harry raced into the forest, hoping to lose them in the shadows. The guards slalomed through the trees and snapped on the xenon flashlights mounted on their machine guns. The shadows disappeared.

But so had Harry. The guards pulled up in a double rooster tail, swinging their lights all around.

A snowbank behind them exploded and Harry moved in like a juggernaut. His fist crunched into the nearest guard's head, just below his ear. The force broke the man's neck. Harry ripped a ski pole out of his lifeless hand and lunged at the second guard, who was trying to turn around, hampered by his skis. A squish and a scream. The pole's point lodged deep in the man's eye socket. Harry anesthetized him with a kick to the side of the head, then reloaded his Glock. He looked up toward the chateau and saw he was going to need every twelve-shot clip he had.

Teams of snow-suited security men vomited out of the chateau's service gate, some on skis, some on snowmobiles.

Harry threw himself down the hill, knees pumping high, plowing through the snow. He couldn't see the road, but he knew it was close. But so were the snowmobiles. Harry glanced over his shoulder: There were a dozen separate light sources probing through the trees. And each light source was a bullet source.

"Gib—" said Harry, but he never finished his thought. One of the light beams found him and a hail of bullets followed, splintering wood, tearing up the snow all around him, turning the slope into a cloud of white powder.

Harry cut into the cloud. Momentarily hidden from view, he stopped and turned, letting the guards overrun his position. By the time they saw him, it was too late. Harry fired his Glock. *Blam Blam*. Two trigger-happy skiers went to a place where there is no snow. *Blam Blam*. A snowmobile driver luckily died before he hit the rock that ignited his fuel tank. *Blam Blam.* Two skiers lost their edges and kissed unforgiving trees.

Harry bolted, cutting across the grain of their onslaught. He found a steeper and—he hoped— faster slope to the road. It turned out much faster than he thought. He lost his footing the first second, fell ass over elbows, and began sliding uncontrollably down the hill headfirst and on his back.

Harry's misfortune didn't stop anyone from shooting at him or trying to run him over with a snowmobile. So as Harry hurtled down the mountain like a human toboggan, he found himself returning fire from his mobile, but supine position. *Blam Blam Blam. Blam Blam Blam.* The guards died very surprised.

Gib spun the van into an icy turn, deftly keeping traction through the hairy slide. He looked upslope at the waving lights and gunfire. Harry was obviously alive, but all Gib could hear on the subvocal was a dull, faraway *thwack* of gunfire and Harry's panting and grunting.

"Harry, what's your twenty? I need a position, buddy—"

Gib's foot hit the brake as a sled wearing a tuxedo crashed through the brush at the edge of the slope and launched out over the road. Gib heard a subvocal "Oof!" and knew it was Harry who had just hit the icy asphalt.

Harry slid across the path of the van and plowed into the snow piled on the shoulder of the road.

Gib's braking distance took him several yards past Harry, so he watched the mirror on Faisil's side as

Harry stood up, brushed the snow off his tux, then sauntered toward the van, looking mildly annoyed. Something about the scene made Gib chuckle.

Harry walked up to Faisil's window. "Lean back," he said.

Gib and Faisil looked momentarily puzzled, but quickly leaned back as Harry's Glock came up and fired through their open windows. *Blam Blam Blam.*

Khaled's security patrol lost its two slowest skiers.

"Let's go," said Harry, opening Faisil's door. "We can still make our flight."

TWO

As the American Airlines 747 touched down at Dulles, Harry was looking out the window, thinking about his father, Fritz Tasker. During World War II, Fritz's comrades in the French Resistance had code-named him "The Wolf." And though he'd begged for something less dramatic, like "The Weasel," they had insisted. As Harry knew well, a wolf was much closer to the mark.

At age twenty-five, Fritz was an Austrian conscript working as a squad leader for the German occupation forces in Yugoslavia. One night his company was tipped off to a behind-the-lines parachute drop of Allied OSS agents. The tip was accurate: Many of the agents were machine-gunned in the air, and most of the rest were hunted down and summarily executed. But five of them hid in a sod-covered creamery cellar, and it was Fritz who found them there. He didn't give them away. To him they weren't the enemy, they were the living embodiment of resistance to Nazi rule. They would also prove to be his ticket to the other side.

He returned under cover of darkness and led the men on a 400-mile journey out of Yugoslavia, across the Nazi stronghold of his native Austria, and through Switzerland into free France. For the duration of the war he worked with the Resistance, headquartered in the tiny fishing village of Yvoire on the south shore of Lake Geneva. Yvoire was one of the key stations on the underground railroad running out of occupied France and Eastern Europe. Fritz and his comrades saved the lives of countless downed airmen, local partisans, and others fleeing the crushing heel of the Nazis.

After the war, Fritz moved to Dover, Delaware, became a U.S. citizen, and started up an international airfreight company. The ensuing years passed uneventfully for Fritz's family. But shortly before he died, Fritz took his college-age son, Harry, on a mysterious trip to France. Fritz was proud of his son. Harry was an all-American in track and football, a brilliant scholar, and beneath his wolfish grin, a man as driven and cunning as his father. But Fritz thought there was something important his son didn't know—a sense of what his life *cost*. An understanding of how much courage, how many ultimate sacrifices it took to provide him with the opportunities he enjoyed.

Father and son drove to Yvoire and stopped for dinner at a seafood dive run by one of his dad's elderly Resistance friends, Frank Hébert. His dad and old Hébert told him about their experiences during the war. It took them all night, but Harry never felt sleepy. Along about dawn, his father dropped the real bombshell. His airfreight company was a front. Ever since the war, Fritz had been working covert operations for the CIA. And that was that. Fritz never said another word on the subject.

He died not long afterward. For years, the scene when they left Yvoire kept replaying in Harry's mind. All the elderly men of the village and their grown sons and daughters turned out and embraced old Fritz. This was the last time they would see him, and they cried, and their tears said "We can never thank you enough."

In college, and throughout graduate school in theoretical physics, Harry kept thinking, Who would cry when he left? Who would embrace him for having lived the life he planned to live?

Then one day, Harry was amusing some classmates by sketching a design for a hydrogen bomb he swore he could whip up in his garage. The only difficult part was the plutonium, and that wasn't so hard to get anymore, right? They all laughed about it, but later, after his friends had left, Harry stared at his drawing a long time and realized it wasn't a joke.

He made some calculations. A crude little one-kiloton bomb would be compact enough to transport in a VW Bug. A bomb like that, set off in a densely populated city, would wipe out maybe two million human beings. He looked around him. The campus commons was crowded with young people, most working hard to make a decent future for themselves and for the generation after them. Harry suddenly realized there was a new, very clear, and very present danger to everything he saw around him.

The next morning Harry bought a plane ticket to Washington, took a taxi to CIA headquarters in

Langley, and started talking to the first person who would listen. When he walked out, the course of his life had changed.

"Hey, time to go, buddy," said Gib, tossing him his overnight bag. Harry stood up and joined his friend in the jetliner's aisle.

An hour later, Gib was driving Harry and himself to their homes in a middle-class suburb of Bethesda. It was cold and wet outside, deep in October, and the streets were strewn with damp, gusting leaves.

The houses they passed were all neat and two stories high, with trimmed lawns, straight hedges, and trees in fall colors. These were houses that looked like homes, like places where families could, if they would, find cozy solace, and live their whole lives feeling they had made good on the promise that was America.

Gib pulled over in front of a house that looked just like all the others. But this house made Harry smile. He was home, the one place he could count on not to explode in flames under him.

Harry sighed and began emptying his pockets: passport, business cards, credit cards, plane tickets—anything with the name Renquist on it. He dropped them all in a zip-lock bag Gib held out to him, then double-checked all his pockets.

"Empty. Go."

Gib started handing him items from a briefcase between them. It was an old routine.

"Harry Tasker wallet. Harry Tasker passport. Plane ticket stub, hotel receipt, Tasker. Two post-cards of Lake Geneva. House keys. Souvenir showing Swiss village."

Gib showed him how it snows when you shake it up and turn it over.

"What's that for?"

"For Dana, schmuck. Bring your kid something. You know. The dad thing."

"Got it. Nice touch," said Harry, opening his door. "Pick me up at eight. The debrief is at ten hundred."

"Hey, hey, hey . . . What are we forgetting?" Gib held up a gold wedding band.

Harry took it and put it on. "What a team." He grinned. "See you at eight."

"Yup. Sleep fast." Gib watched his buddy go a moment, then sped away.

Harry let himself in. It was four A.M. and people are pretty hard to wake at that hour, but Harry was careful to be quiet anyway. He put down his suitcase and walked along the hall till he came to a door plastered anarchically with lurid stickers and signs: STAY OUT! TOXIC WASTE. IF IT'S TOO LOUD YOU'RE TOO OLD.

Harry silently opened the door and looked in at his sleeping daughter, Dana. For the second time in twenty-four hours, Harry's breath was taken away. But it wasn't his daughter's innocent beauty that awed him, it was the inexplicable, diaphanous glow emanating from her pale face and flaxen hair. He glanced over her bed. The window was curtained; no moonlight came through; yet her face glowed, literally, like an angel's. Harry rubbed his eyes. Was this some kind of miracle? He moved closer, toward the face that, besides his wife's, he loved more than any other in the world; toward the face that was about a foot away from a small television lying on its side and tuned silently to MTV.

Harry smiled ruefully and let out a relieved sigh. Like most people who have had a near-miracle experience, he suddenly realized that miracles were a huge pain in the ass.

Harry switched off the glowing tube. X rays from the tiny CRT had no doubt fried a few thousand of her neurons by now but, proud father that he was, he figured she had plenty to spare. Glow or no glow, to Harry she would always be an angel, the one and only absolutely unflawed person on the planet.

But Dana was hardly an angel. She was a complex, yearning, frustrated fourteen-year-old, torn by the irresistible hormonal and social crosscurrents buffeting her from every direction. And Harry Tasker, superspy, was a clueless dad. He tiptoed silently out and closed the door.

The lump in the balled-up covers did not stir when Harry came into the room. Helen Tasker, Harry's wife of fifteen years, was used to his ghosting in at odd hours. She had long since given up waiting or worrying. Harry worked so hard; he was so loyal— there was nothing to worry *about*. Harry was Harry, solid as a sequoia.

Harry slipped into the bed. He kissed her tenderly on the cheek and she stirred. She rolled toward him and gave him a sleepy hug, kissing him and mewling.

"Hi, honey," she murmured, rolling away again. "How was the flight?"

"Fine, honey. Stay asleep."

"Okay." And she drifted off.

Harry laid his head back on the pillow and consciously relaxed every muscle in his body. He marvelled that he had what every man wanted but not many got. A great job . . . nice house . . . loving family . . . Gib was coming at eight . . . The transcripts from Khaled's computer were being transcribed. . . . Harry drifted off, images of ghostly, onrushing skiers making him twist in his sleep.

"You shake it up," boomed Harry, shouting over the profane hip-hop that seemed to pressurize his daughter's room.

Dana shook the snow globe. She noticed that the tiny Swiss moron waving from inside the snowstorm had a grin on his face exactly like her dad's.

"Hey, thanks, Dad," she said, "I never had one of these."

"You're welcome, pumpkin." Harry bent and kissed her on the cheek, then checked his watch. "You better hurry. You'll be late for school. And don't forget to feed Gizmo," he said, indicating the greasy dust mop beside her, which was actually the family dog.

Dana nodded, making a "Have A Nice Day" face: "Okay, Dad."

One last smile from Harry and he was thankfully on his way, crushing CD covers with his giant brown shoes, stepping on something that squeaked, twisting his ankle on a pair of her army boots. His foot slid on a short stack of glossy magazines, and he fell toward the wall. He threw out an arm to steady himself, but withdrew it quickly when he noticed his palm was spread over Eddie Vedder's crotch.

Dana watched her dad stumble gratefully out the door. There was a turbulent storm in her heart she couldn't articulate. Her brow knitted and her throat tightened painfully. Why would her dad's gift make her feel *bad*? Sure it was lame, but there was something else. He'd *given* her something, but she felt ripped off. Gizmo barked sharply. Dana tossed the snow globe with its grinning Swiss burgher into the circular file.

"I'm late," said Harry, breezing into the master bedroom.

"Me, too," said Helen, dropping her terrycloth robe.

Harry didn't even look at her. He didn't realize it, but he had long ago moved her from the pedestal to the mantelpiece, which was a terrible waste, because Helen was a smart, funny, and very attractive woman. She wore glasses sometimes, kept her hair plain and short, used only perfunctory makeup—but an unjaded eye would have noticed her long-limbed grace, her mischievous, full mouth, and the brave, optimistic sparkle in her eye.

Helen pulled on a blouse, checking her outfit in the full-length mirror. If she'd looked deeper, she would have seen a well-adjusted person, someone who held herself responsible for her own happiness and fulfillment. She had always taken care of herself, done what she wanted to do, courageously and with all her heart. When she had left Georgetown Law School at the end of her first year to have a child with Harry, her "friends" had been appalled, dismissive. Many times in the last few weeks of her studies, she heard the wedding march, baby talk, and derisive giggles echoing down the halls behind her. But she had wanted a child; and though that dawning desire surprised her as much as it did her friends, she didn't try to intellectualize it away; she just did it.

When she was six, she had spent a summer in North Carolina with her mother's mother. They were sitting on the porch one day, still getting to know each other, and Grams said, "You wanna see somethin'?" Helen nodded, her big eyes staring up. Grams reached into her mouth and pulled out her choppers, a full set, uppers and lowers, then placed them on the porch swing between them. As an adult, Helen always wondered how Grams knew a little girl would love that so much. Nowadays, she'd probably lose her lunch. But as a child, she had stared in absolute wonder, then broke into a big grin that Grams had toothlessly echoed.

And it was Grams who had told her many times, "You do what your heart tells you. Listen carefully, listen slow, but do it."

And so she had, always, honoring her Gram's memory with complete trust in herself, and a will of iron. She had stayed home with her daughter till Dana started pre-school, then done volunteer legal work for several years, setting her own hours. When Dana entered her pre-teens and no longer needed or wanted her around, Helen had taken her present job as a paralegal in the D.C. law firm of Kettleman Barnes & McGrath. As a paralegal she was able to do everything a lawyer did, but still be home for dinner. She received neither the glory nor salary of the licensed lawyers, but she did have the satisfaction of the work, and a big share of the responsibility for whether a case was won or lost. And once Dana left home, Helen would finish her law degree, and dedicate her life to that.

Helen gave her hair a quick brush. "How'd it go at the trade show? You make all the other salesmen jealous?"

"Yeah, you should have seen it. We were the hit of the show with the new model ordering system, the one for the 680 . . . how you can write up an order and the second the customer's name goes into the computer, it starts checking their credit, and if they've ordered anything in the past, and if they get a discount . . ."

Helen was already tuning him out, checking her teeth for lipstick stains. A dull regret, faraway and quickly smothered, tugged at her breast. Perhaps there was one little murmur from her heart she wasn't listening to. She found herself sighing, checking her purse, her mood weighed down by a feeling concocted of equal parts exhaustion and affection. She missed Harry when he was gone, and often regretted that his job, designing and installing corporate computer systems, took him away so often. But when he was home, she realized, he was—there was no other word for it—dull. A good man, a man she would always love, but boooooring.

She noticed he'd stopped talking and quickly said, "That's fabulous, Harry," then went into the bathroom.

"Yeah it was wild," Harry said, smiling. As usual, the lies were giving him a warm feeling all over.

Gib opened Harry's front door and strode in, not bothering to knock until he was entering the living room.

"Morning!" he announced unnecessarily, then turned sharply as a barking hairball attacked him: It was Gizmo looking about as scary as a fake mustache. Gib, glaring through a mean pair of black Ray-Bans, growled at the tiny, stupid, and legless end-product of whimsical breeding experiments.

"Come any closer and I'll kill you."

Gizmo whined and scurried away, alerting his masters to the invasion, and incidentally cleaning the hallway floor.

Gib threw his jacket over the back of a chair, then carefully positioned a pack of cigarettes on the mantelpiece. On close inspection, a tiny lens was visible at one end of the pack. Gib positioned it to cover the room and walked out toward the kitchen.

Meanwhile, back in the master bedroom, it was Harry's turn to tune out.

"The plumber came yesterday," Helen called out from the bathroom.

Harry knotted his tie, eyes glazing over. "What did he want?"

"I called *him*. The kitchen drain, remember?"

"Uh-huh."

"He said they have to dig under the slab or something and it's going to be six hundred dollars to fix."

"Okay."

Helen walked back into the bedroom. "It's not okay. It's extortion."

"Right."

"But I slept with him and he knocked off a hundred bucks."

Harry straightened his tie, turned to his wife, and gave her a peck good-bye. "Good thinking, honey." And he was gone.

Helen buttoned her blazer, staring unfocused into

space. Then she kissed the air where Harry had been.

Gib entered the kitchen, heading for the coffeepot. Dana stood holding the fridge open, guzzling orange juice straight from the carton. A giant motorcycle helmet was tipped back on her head.

"Hi, kid."

"Hey, Gib. What up?" She pulled the helmet down.

"Boy, I remember the first time I got shot out of a cannon."

Dana rolled her eyes. Nothing a computer wonk said could possibly be witty. She grabbed a Pop Tart, waved, and was gone.

Harry came in a second later, and Gib handed him a cup of coffee.

"Thanks, dear."

Gib handed Harry his Ray-Bans. "Check it out."

Harry saw a black-and-white video image of his living room projected on the inside of the left lens.

"The CCD camera and transmitter are inside a pack of smokes on your mantel. Slick little unit, huh?"

Harry slipped the glasses on. He could see his immediate surroundings and his living room, both in sharp focus.

"*Very* slick."

Harry continued watching as Dana entered the living room. He watched her go straight to Gib's jacket, fish out his wallet, and remove two twenties in a blink of an eye.

"Son of a bitch!"

"What?" said Gib.

"She's ripping you off!"

Harry whipped off the glasses and charged out of the kitchen.

"I knew it," said Gib, following more slowly.

"Dana—!"

But Dana was already out the front door and slamming it behind her. She ran down the lawn and leapt onto the back of a little high-revving Yamaha, tricked out with cape and faring, and piloted by her sixteen-year-old, grunge clone boyfriend, Trent.

Harry burst out the front door, still bellowing: "Dana!"

Trent popped the clutch, tore up a patch of lawn, and shot into the street.

Dana waved. "Can't stop! I'm late! 'Bye, Dad!"

The bike disappeared down the street, throwing up a rooster tail of red and yellow leaves.

Harry stared after Dana in total disbelief. His angel. The apple of his eye. She had palmed those twenties like a pro. Harry looked dazed. A vise was squeezing his chest.

"Kids," Gib said, steering his gray Jimmy into the heart of downtown D.C. "Ten seconds of joy. Thirty years of misery."

"She knows not to steal," said Harry, unappeased. "We taught her better than that."

"Yeah, but you're not her parents anymore. Her parents are Axl Rose and Madonna. The five minutes you spend with her every day can't compete with that kind of bombardment. You're outgunned, amigo."

Gib swung the car onto Pennsylvania Avenue, heading toward Lafayette Square. Capitol Hill was behind them; ahead the White House and the Ellipse, within which were all the national monuments that memorialized the ideas and way of life Harry strove to protect. For the sake of his child. A child who had somehow learned to steal. Harry Tasker was at a loss for what to do.

The Jimmy entered the parking structure underneath an unremarkable glass-and-steel office building on one of D.C.'s letter streets. It was headquarters to several import-export companies, lobbyists' offices, law partnerships and CPAs, a couple of bail bondsmen and insurance companies, and one computer systems designer, Tektel Systems, which took up the twelfth floor.

Harry and Gib stepped out of the elevator and greeted the receptionist, striding off between the grid of rectangular cubicles that filled the floor as far as one could see. Everyone went about their very real business as the boys walked by, continuing a conversation muted by a low ceiling of acoustical tiles and a soft carpeted floor.

"See, kids now are ten years ahead of where we were at the same age. You probably think she's still a virgin."

"Don't be ridiculous. She's only—How old is she?"

"Fourteen."

"Right. She's only fourteen."

They turned into a corridor. "Uh-huh. And her little hormones are going like a fire alarm. I say even money that physicist on the bike is boinking her."

"No way! Not Dana."

They stopped at a door. Like all the others along the corridor, it was unmarked. "Okay, okay," said Gib, "De-nial ain't just a river in Egypt."

"Will you just open the door!"

Gib touched a plastic card to an unmarked spot on the jamb. A hidden solenoid switch thunked, opening an internal lock. Harry turned the knob and pushed the door open.

Gib nodded to himself. "She's probably stealing the money to pay for an abortion."

Harry, walking through, looked over his shoulder to stare daggers at his friend.

"Or drugs," said Gib, following. The door thunked closed behind them.

They walked down a long featureless corridor. Cameras panned and zoomed, centered on their moving forms. You got the distinct impression that this was some kind of transition tunnel leading from one world to the next.

"Twenty here, fifty there," Gib said, innocently continuing his torture, "For a while, I figured my wife's scumbag boyfriend was taking it."

"I thought you moved out."

"Well, I moved back in. My lawyer said it would give me a better claim on the house in the property settlement. Don't change the subject. You owe me two hundred bucks."

Harry's eyes bulged.

They approached another door, this one with a bulletproof window in it. On the other side of the door, in a brightly lit room containing only a desk and a bank of monitors, an unsmiling, aggressively homely woman sat peering at multiperspective X-ray images of Harry and Gib. Her name was Janice, but many of her co-workers referred to her as "Pumice." No one ever joked like that in front of her however, any more than they would joke in front of Cerberus

at the Gates of Hell. Janice was lethal and utterly
focused on her job. As she buzzed the boys in, her
hand closed around the butt and trigger of a .45
tucked in a well-oiled holster riveted to the underside
of her desk.

Harry and Gib stepped into Janice's icy domain.
"Morning, Janice," said Gib with a suave wink. No
one ever joked . . . except for Gib. To this date Janice
hadn't shot him, and Gib bragged far and wide
that this was evidence of her romantic infatuation
with him.

"Gentlemen, please identify yourselves to the
scanner."

The two men stepped up to a wall-mounted scanner unit, bent and peered into eye-pieces, placed
their thumbs on plates of black glass, and identified
themselves verbally. Thus they were simultaneously
identified by retinal scan, thumbprint, and voice-
print.

"Harry Tasker. One zero zero two four."

"Albert Gibson. Three four nine nine one."

Janice watched their clearance flash on a monitor
in front of her. Only then did she take her hand off
the .45.

"Thank you," said Janice, handing them their
plastic ID badges.

"Janice," said Gib, "How many years have you
been buzzing us in?"

"Ten, Mr. Gibson."

"And you still reach for your piece every time."

"Yes, sir."

"God! You have no idea how much that turns
me on."

Harry dragged Gib away, through a heavy steel door that opened with a pneumatic hiss.

They walked across a cylindrical room, which was actually an airtight sally port. Two Marines stood still as mannequins behind a Lexan shield, their MP5's held steady and ready. An oval design was inlaid in the marble floor: an ellipse surrounding the Greek letter omega, which in turn surrounded the reticle of a target rifle's scope. This was the logo of Omega Sector, whose motto was spelled out on the scroll beneath the logo: The Last Line of Defense.

Harry and Gib exited the sally port and entered the cool blue and gray headquarters of Omega Sector. Unlike their cover firm, Tektel, the workstations were arranged radially and in semicircular clusters. Workers shared curving wraparound command consoles that combined writing surfaces, keyboards, telecommunications equipment, and overhead monitors. The monitors showed everything from CNN to satellite orbits, stock exchange information to decompiled computer code. No one seemed to be hurrying, but there was a sense of utmost urgency, of tremendous hushed power. And underneath it all, the smooth, silky, subliminal rush of terabytes of information.

Fast Faisil leaned back in his chair and yawned as Harry and Gib strode by.

Without breaking step, Harry said, "Come on, Fize. We're late for our butt-grinding."

Faisil spun in his chair.

"Wait, Harry. He's in with the new recruits. You have to give your speech."

Harry checked his watch, looking at the date. "Oh right. Come on then." He altered course for the lecture hall. Faisil grabbed his coffee, started to follow—

Harry called back, "Put on your jacket. Set an example, for godsake."

Faisil grabbed his jacket and hurried after them.

As the three men quietly let themselves into the lecture hall, a ceremony was in progress. Twelve young men and women had their right hands raised and were repeating the words intoned by a tall, lean, rawboned man standing at the lectern below.

Spencer Trilby, Chief of Omega Sector, was definitely the man in charge. His aquiline face was slashed diagonally by a black strap and an oddly small eyepatch. Having lost one eye seemed only to have intensified the other, which glittered with such concentrated energy that most of the agents at Omega Sector found themselves hypnotized if they stared at it too long. And then there was his soft Carolina drawl, perfectly suited for both genteel courtesy and quiet death threats.

Chief Trilby finished his reading of the Omega Sector oath. ". . . and the security of this nation, so help me God."

". . . So help me God," intoned the recruits.

"At ease, ladies and gentlemen. You may be seated."

The recruits sighed with relief, looked at each other with smothered delight, and took their seats.

Trilby let his eye roam over each and every one of them. "You are now members of Omega Sector. Your mission is the interdiction of nuclear terrorism, through whatever means necessary. Let me say that again: *Whatever means necessary.*" The Chief paused, and again stared at each of them.

Harry, Gib, and Faisil remembered the thrill they felt when they had first heard those words, the flush of freedom and terror that had filled their bodies. The Chief always paused after that line, not just for dramatic effect, but to let something else sink in: the enormous responsibility that came with total license.

The Chief continued: "Omega Sector has no Congressional oversight. You will not find a budget for it anywhere in the G.O.A.'s annual report. You answer to one man. Me. And I answer to one man, and that's the President. Officially, we do not exist. But if Omega Sector were to call an alert, any of you could commandeer the resources of any branch of the armed forces, or any federal agency, instantly and without question."

The recruits, the best and the brightest skimmed from intelligence and law-enforcement agencies, from the military, NASA, and postgraduate university programs, all had heard rumors about Omega Sector's mission and mandate, but this was the first time it had been stated to them officially, and somehow it came as a shock and surprise.

"You are here because you are the best," Trilby continued. "You will begin your advanced training today, to become the *best* of the best. I'm going to turn you over now to Senior Agent Harry Tasker." Trilby nodded to Harry, who was seated way at the back.

Harry got up from his seat, his glare discouraging the curious stares of the recruits.

"Give 'em hell, Harry," Gib whispered.

Trilby continued: "Harry has been with Omega

Sector almost since its formation seventeen years ago. Like many of you he was recruited directly from college. He is one of our finest field agents. He holds postgraduate degrees in physics and engineering, speaks seven languages, and he can shoot the eye out of a crow at sixty yards." Trilby nodded to Harry and stepped away from the dais.

But Harry didn't mount the stage. He turned along the first row, walking right in front of the seated recruits, frankly sizing them up.

Harry began quietly, making them listen carefully. "Any concept you have of your work here must begin with an understanding of your opponent. Your opponent at eyeball level—not the string pullers, or ideologues, or intelligence professionals behind them, but the water carrier. He is a man who is willing to drive a car with a nuclear weapon in it into one of our cities and then set it off. By hand. He is not reasonable or rationally motivated. He is inflamed by the sacred religious texts, by the promise of the millennium, by the illusions of quick justice and retribution. He is tireless. And he is willing to die for what he believes."

Harry tilted his head and looked hard at the young woman seated closest to him. "Are you?"

He moved on, peering into another face. "How about you?" Without waiting for an answer, Harry moved on, knowing that each and every one of them was even then, silently pledging their lives.

"In the years ahead, some of you may lose your lives. And all of you will lose part of your lives— because you can never tell the truth to the people you love. You can't whisper it in their ears, you can't

mumble about it in your sleep, and you can't blurt it
out during a shit-faced crying jag."

Gib smiled bitterly. Having gone down in flames
three times on the family front, he knew better than
most the cost of being wedded to Omega Sector. Few
Omega veterans had intact marriages. After one or
two painful failures, many decided to live their lives
as singles.

Harry continued: "For your safety and security,
even those closest to you will never know about your
work here. Sharing the accomplishments and the
wounds of life with a wife or husband or lover is one
of the big reasons we *have* wives, husbands, and
lovers. *You* can't do it. You will live in a web of lies.
But you will be guided by the one important truth:
You truly are the last line of defense."

Harry fell silent and paced a moment, letting his
words sink in. Then he turned and faced them, both
hands in his pockets, looking deceptively casual.
"You have passed through the looking glass. There is
no going back. Omega Sector is not the place you
work, it is the purpose of your life."

Time for their butt-grinding. Harry, Gib, and Faisil
strode manfully toward Trilby's office. Well, at least
Harry did.

The old man eyed them coldly as they approached,
sitting there like a spider at the center of his web.
This was no metaphor: Trilby's "office" was set in
the exact physical center of Omega Sector. It was
not walled off in any way, and consisted of a single
thirty-foot circular workstation that surrounded a
Cray 3-MP. A cluster of giant monitors leaned down
from the ceiling directly over the Cray. Trilby's

secretary and assistants sat at consoles all around the station.

Trilby himself sat at the far end of a small conference table jutting radially into the surrounding space.

"Good morning, sir," said Harry, as they took their seats. Faisil grabbed a wireless notepad lying on the table, and began retrieving data from his file server, routing it to the big screen behind Trilby.

Trilby gave them the fish eye. "Jesus, Harry. You guys really screwed the pooch last night. Please tell me how I can look at this, that it's not a total pooch-screw."

Harry seemed to be making a strenuous mental effort: "*Total* is a strong word—"

"There are degrees of totality," chimed in Gib.

"It's a scale really," Faisil said hopefully. "With perfect mission on one end, and total pooch-screw on the other, and we're more about here—"

Trilby skewered Faisil with his laser-beam gaze, almost giving Fize a heart attack.

"Faisil," Trilby drawled menacingly, "you're new on Harry's team, aren't you?"

"Y-y-yes, sir."

"So what makes you think that the slack I cut him in *any* way translates to you?"

"Sorry, sir. Uhm . . . here's what we got." Faisil nodded encouragingly toward the big monitor behind Trilby, extremely relieved when that glittering eye turned away and looked at the screen.

"Jamel Khaled," said Faisil, naming the man whose photo filled one side of the screen. "We know that two weeks ago, four MIRV warheads were smuggled out of the former Soviet republic of Kazakhstan. We also know there are only a few potential buyers. We accessed their accounts . . ." Fize glanced at Harry. ". . . one way or another. There was no significant activity in the North Korean's Swiss accounts. Ditto for the Libyans. Then we found this . . ."

Faisil's fingers pitter-patted on the notepad's muted keys.

A spreadsheet opened on the screen, a single entry highlighted in a square of yellow.

Faisil continued: "One hundred million dollars transferred from Khaled's account at the Commerce Bank International."

Gib piped up: "An account we all know is a front for *certain* nations to fund terrorist activities."

Harry tied it up: "Chief, we think Khaled's group has bought the nukes."

Trilby thought it over a moment, then turned to look at them. "So far this is not blowing my skirt up, gentlemen. A hundred million dollars would also buy the Oak Hills Country Club in Georgetown. Who did the money go to?"

Gib shook his head. "Sir, it's an unidentified debit, but that in itself is suspicious."

"Don't be pumping beets up my ass here, Gib. Do you have hard data?"

Harry piped up, deflecting the heat onto himself: "No sir. Not what you'd call *rock hard* . . ."

"It's pretty limp, actually," mumbled Gib.

Trilby sighed. "Well get some . . . before somebody parks a car in front of the White House with a nuclear weapon in the trunk."

The Washington law firm of Kettleman Barnes & McGrath had 227 attorneys, all feeding out of the government trough either directly or indirectly. There were contracts to be drawn up with government departments, bids to be submitted to this or that agency, lawsuits to be brought, politicians to be defended, prosecutions to stall—all paid for out of the taxpayer's pocket, a pocket so deep that though all 227 lawyers rooted and snorfled hour after billable hour, they never seemed to find the bottom.

Helen Tasker deplored the waste. Someday she'd be in a position to do something about it, but for now she enjoyed the fact that she was working hard, learning every day, and had for the most part, pleasant colleagues to pass the time with.

Her best friend and coffee-break companion was Allison Dawkins, younger, single, and always curious about married life.

Helen, as usual, was enlightening her. "It's not like he's saving the world or anything. He's a sales rep for Chrissakes. Whenever I can't get to sleep I ask him to tell me about his day. Six seconds and I'm out. But he acts like he's curing cancer or something."

Allison thought she saw the thorn in Helen's paw. "So I guess you didn't get away for the weekend after all?"

"Are you kidding?" Helen said. "Harry had to go out of town."

"I'm shocked," said Allison, miming that very emotion.

"Yeah. You know Harry."

Allison wished she did, so she could smack him upside his pointy head. She and Helen had always kept their ragging at the level of a joke, but Allison had seen the underlying tension and hurt eating away at Helen lately, becoming more and more obvious with each passing month. At least it was obvious to Allison. Helen, she knew, was trying to convince herself her life with Harry really *was* amusing; she was trying to accept her neglect, see it as an unexpected, but inescapable part of mature married life. Allison revolted at the thought.

One of the lawyers that Helen assisted, quintessentially named Brad, walked up behind her, his face miserable, and his voice a nasal whine: "Helen, did you prepare those briefs yet? I need them by lunch, I really do."

Helen turned and froze the helpless youngster with a quiet, sadistic smile. "Do you know what time it is, Brad?"

"Um . . . I . . ."

"It's my *break-time*."

Brad gaped a moment, hoping for at least a little reassurance. None was forthcoming. He mewled unhappily and walked away.

"Little pencil-neck," said Helen. "They've been sitting in his in-tray for an hour."

Allison laughed. Helen was feared by the firm's lesser lawyers. She took no prisoners as far as they were concerned. Allison wished her friend would take a little of that bad attitude home with her. She'd suggested it before, but her exhortations only elicited high-pitched defenses of Harry—his sweetness, loyalty, dedication, blah blah blah.

Coffees creamed and sugared, the two women headed back to their adjoining cubicles, continuing their typical Monday conversation.

Helen asked, "So, yo sista', you do anything interesting this weekend?"

Allison had been dreading that question for several
minutes now, but suddenly she decided to give it to
Helen with both barrels.

"Oh . . . Eric and I drove up to this little romantic
inn, and pretty much lapped champagne out of each
other's navels for two days."

"You *bitch!*"

"Girlfriend"—Allison laughed—"You got a man.
You just have to take control. Set up the right mood."

"Harry only has two moods. Busy and asleep."

"Then you better do something to jump-start that
man's motor. Wake up the sleeping giant of his
passion."

That made Helen chuckle.

Allison continued her prescription: "You slap him
awake, tell him he's got work to do. Make this
mama suffer!"

That sent Helen over the top.

Crossing the Omega Sector data centers, Harry met
up with Gib and Faisil coming from the Analysis
Department. They fell into step on either side of
him.

Faisil handed Harry a printout. "Check this out."

Gib's face was intent. He smelled blood. "It's
a two-million-dollar disbursement from Khaled to
Juno Skinner."

Harry raised an eyebrow.

Gib nodded. "Uh-huh, the babe at the party."

Harry handed the printout back. "It doesn't mean
anything. She buys antiquities for Khaled."

Gib shook his head. "Nope. The art buys are in a
separate ledger."

Faisil agreed. "And this is a little above market

rate for the horizontal bop, even for a total biscuit like her."

Harry tried not to think of Juno and the horizontal bop. He put her . . . very *palpable* attractions out of his mind, and considered the situation objectively.

"All right. I want a complete workout on her—I mean, workup." Harry glowered at Gib, daring him to laugh.

Gib clamped his jaw tight.

Harry collected his dignity and continued, "Do we know where she is?"

"Right here in River City," said Faisil.

Harry felt his heart flop over with a thump. "You're kidding," he said, an edge of terror in his voice.

"She lives in Rome, but she does stuff with the Smithsonian and has a lot of diplomatic connections. She has offices over on Constitution."

Harry stopped at his personal workstation, picked up some papers, affecting distraction. He made sure to sound utterly dour, totally professional, as he said, "I need to get inside there." Harry glanced narrowly at his comrades. "In her offices."

Gib bit down hard on his lower lip, then sighed, turned to the straight-faced Faisil, and said, "Sounds like a job for a specialist. Do you dance?"

Gib and Faisil swirled away locked cheek to cheek in a tango.

Harry turned to his desk. "Assholes."

Three

From abacuses to computers, handguns to F-16's, Harry Tasker was trained and battle tested on almost any device you could name. But the device he had more hours with than any other, the one he could operate blindfolded, was the microwave.

Ding!

Harry didn't realize it, but that sound actually made him salivate.

Harry swallowed unconsciously, his fingers blindly searching for and pressing the button that opened the microwave. He removed the plate, elbowed the door shut, then gingerly removed the plastic wrap Helen had so conscientiously covered his dinner with—all without taking his eyes off the sports page.

Harry, like most men when they're alone, ate like a disgusting pig. His meaty fist closed around a chicken leg-and-thigh combination and brought the tender, dripping meat toward his mouth. It might as well have been a boar's haunch the way he grunted and tore at it.

Helen walked in unexpectedly, right in the middle of one of Harry's more paleolithic grunts. Harry froze, chicken veins hanging out the side of his mouth. He swallowed, then demurely reached for a napkin.

"Enjoying yourself I see," said Helen, drolly. "I need you to talk to Dana. The vice-principal called. She cut classes again this afternoon."

Harry, disappointed, laid his chicken haunch on the plate and stood up, wiping his hands.

"I'll handle it," he said, and headed for the back door.

Dana dribbled the ball from hand to hand, talking trash to an imaginary opponent.

"You can't guard me. Sucker. Get out my face." Dana busted half a move, threw up a brick, and bobbled the rebound.

But she didn't lose an ounce of attitude. She faced her nemesis again.

"You ain't shi—"

"Dana."

Dana turned as her dad walked up. She threw him the ball. "Take a shot, Dad."

But Harry held on to the ball and stopped directly in front of her.

"Mr. Hardy called. Why weren't you in class today?"

"He lies! I was there! I was in the nurse's office, 'cause I had a headache."

"You seem fine now."

"Oh, great! You're going to believe that dweeb Mr. Hardy over your own daughter."

Harry felt an unpleasant gloom, realizing she was correct. Two days ago, he would've trusted Dana.

"I'm not sure what to believe anymore, young lady. You never used to lie to me. But lately you don't seem to know the difference between right and wrong."

Dana studied something really fascinating at the end of her fingernail. But for her pretended insolence, she was suddenly afraid. Her big complaint about her father had always been that he was clueless. Now she suspected he knew things about her that she didn't want him to know, that she never imagined he'd find out.

And the realization of what she must look like to him filled her with shame. She wished he was clueless again! But if he wouldn't have been clueless in the first place, she would never—Oh! Dana's thoughts whirled into confusion. She found her shame suddenly turning to anger.

"Dana, are you listening to me?"

"Yeah, Dad," she said, tight-lipped, wanting him to go away.

"You know you can always talk to me. Right? Whatever is going on in your life, your mom and I will understand."

"Okay."

Harry reached out and put a hand on her shoulder. "You'd tell me if there was something wrong, wouldn't you, pumpkin?"

Dana spun out from under his arm, furious.

"I'm not a *pumpkin*! Okay? Do I look even *remotely* like a pumpkin? I'm not a muffin either, or a cupcake, or a honeybear! And you don't understand *anything*, Dad!"

She ran toward the house, trying not to let him see her cry.

Harry watched her go, mouth hanging open, completely at sea.

Helen stood on the back stoop, holding the screen door open as Dana ran by. She watched her daughter disappear inside, then turned to her husband.

"I'll handle it," said Helen, mocking Harry's deep, macho voice.

A long black limousine slid through the downtown traffic, through a morning full of sunlight and bright promise. Even the honking and cursing from irate motorists had a cheerful, euphonious edge to it today. Or so it seemed to Harry—sitting in the fat-cat seat, popping Smarties from an economy-sized bag, left there by a megaband who'd used the limo that weekend. Today, it was like he was in a musical, and it was just before everyone burst into song. The fact that his lightheartedness had a lot to do with his visit to Juno this morning gave him a twinge of guilt. More like a thrill of guilt, really. He decided to indulge himself. Helen would never know, and nothing would happen, right?

And if Juno was involved with terrorists, well . . . he'd shoot her. They'd always have Switzerland.

"It's all set up," Gib said, dressed in chauffeur's livery, keeping his eyes on the road. "Ghost phones and fax, all the usual stuff. You have the suite at the Marquis Hotel under Renquist. Okay, reality check. Go."

"Hi, I'm Harry Renquist," Harry said in a suave,

manly sort of way. "I own a corporate art consulting
company in San Francisco . . ."

". . . And I have an appointment to see Ms.
Skinner."

Juno's secretary stared at the big, handsome, ele-
gantly dressed hunk, and absently took his business
card.

"Uhm . . . there she is now!"

Juno breezed into the lobby, her eyes going wide
with pleasure.

"Harry!" She took both his hands in hers. "I
thought I might see you again. I just didn't expect
you to call so soon."

"What's the point of waiting?" said Harry, giving
her delicate little fingers a warm squeeze.

"I agree," she said quietly. Their hands and eyes
were still locked.

Juno's secretary gave a little cough.

"Come into the showroom," said Juno. "I've got a
couple of things you might enjoy seeing."

"I'm all eyes."

Somehow Juno had managed to make a stroll
through her first-floor showroom seem like an on-site
archaeological dig. A pair of giant, Assyrian funerary
heads greeted the visitor as he or she walked in the
doors. Fragments of ancient sculpture were propped
slightly askew atop piles of chipped stone. Worn
picks and chipping hammers lay abandoned in front
of hieroglyphic tablets set inside rough-hewn, candlelit wall niches.

Harry was impressed again. Juno showed excep-
tional style in everything she did.

"So your clients want something for their lobby . . ." said Juno, looking over her displays.

"Something dramatic," said Harry. "Everybody said you were the one to see if I wanted a really special piece."

"Oh, really," she said. She led him through a door into a large, high-ceilinged warehouse space. A dozen bustling workmen, mostly Middle Eastern, unpacked large, straw-filled crates. An overhead crane swung heavy stone pieces out of shipping containers.

"And what else did everybody say about me . . . exactly?" Juno headed toward a couple of massive pillars, two stories high, fronting the facade of a 2500-year-old Hittite tomb.

"Let's see," mused Harry. "That you can read ancient Sanskrit without having to sound out the words. And that other dealers and archaeologists don't like you much."

Juno laughed. "Those wimps. That's because I use my diplomatic contacts to export cultural treasures from countries that tell them to take a hike."

Juno noticed two empty crates left out in front of her tomb installation. Switching to Arabic, she yelled at some workmen on a nearby scaffold: "I told you all to move these crates an hour ago! Come on, guys, let's get going!"

The workmen scrambled to obey. All except one: a balding, intense-eyed man in his midthirties, who pretended to continue his work atop the scaffold, never taking his eyes off the couple below.

"You see," continued Juno, "a lot of these pieces are from ancient Persia. Unfortunately, ancient Persia is twenty feet under the sand of Iran, Iraq, and

Syria. Not the most popular places lately. So I've had to become an expert in international diplomacy."

Juno stopped and leaned back against one of the massive pillars. Harry suddenly forgot he was there to look at antiquities. Juno was just as stunning in an ivory wool pantsuit as in an evening gown.

"Do you see anything you like, Mr. Renquist?"

Harry felt a stirring in his sarcophagus.

Harry stared out the wraparound windows of his corner suite at the Marquis Hotel, enjoying the spectacular view of Washington. Everything seemed to make him think of Juno—the Washington Monument, the Capitol Dome . . .

Gib was pointing a finger at Harry, insisting on his point. "You said all her stuff was imported from Middle Eastern countries. All of them unfriendlies. Anything could be in those crates. Guns, money. Anything."

"And the second you left her office," said Faisil, walking by with an electronic scanner, sweeping the suite for listening devices, "we started getting calls to the ghost numbers. They were checking out the Renquist front."

Harry sighed. That was telling. He forced himself once and for all to put Juno in perspective. She was very probably in league with his country's most deadly enemies.

And the Great Satan took a dim view of its enemies.

Harry's dour and professional tone wasn't an act this time. "Okay. Let's step up the surveillance on her. Put on two more guys."

Gib smiled, glad it was all over. He had a hunch

about Juno, or at least he hoped it was a hunch, and not a desperate wish.

Gib had been burning the candle at both ends ever since Trilby called the alert on the four MIRVs. He'd combed dozens of reports sent in by Sector's Middle East assets. Stretching from the Urals to Tangier, Gib knew everything knowable about the movements of bulk contraband in the last two weeks. And he had put together a probable trail for the four MIRVs: from Gurjev on the north shore of the Caspian Sea, down to Iran, then west along the rugged northern borders of Iraq and Syria, to Iskenderun on the Mediterranean coast of Turkey.

Nukes gave off gamma rays almost impossible to hide from the proper scanning equipment. Every ship out of Iskenderun was being checked, and had been for over a week. In fact, every vessel leaving the Med through either the Suez or Gibraltar was being combed with radiation scanners.

But nothing had turned up. Nothing except four, slightly radioactive trucks abandoned on the outskirts of Iskenderun.

The trail was cold.

And that more than worried Gib. It terrified him, and everyone else in Omega Sector. There was no way they could be sure of picking up the trail before a mushroom cloud rose over Philadelphia or Boston Harbor. This was a full alert. And security was total. A leak about four nukes on the way to the West, in the hands of Middle Eastern fanatics, would create a panic almost as unpleasant as an actual detonation.

Nobody in Omega Sector was going on vacation this week.

*   *   *

Juno Skinner looked through her open office door into her reception area. One of her workmen, the intense-eyed man who'd watched her and Harry conversing, bowed self-effacingly to her secretary, then to her, and humbly asked, "Ms. Skinner? Can I speak to you for a moment please?"

The secretary was about to protest, but Juno interrupted her.

"It's all right. Come in, Aziz."

Aziz bowed and smiled at the secretary, then entered Juno's office, closing the door behind him.

Then he straightened up, let his eyes flash, and slapped Juno across the face.

"You stupid, undisciplined bitch!"

Juno took a step backward, flushing with suppressed anger.

"It's a good thing you pay me well," she said touching her cheek.

Aziz moved right up in her face. "Do you realize that there are surveillance teams watching this place right now? Your phones are almost certainly tapped. And you are busy laughing and flirting like a whore with this Renquist, who may be a—"

"No, he checked out okay—"

Aziz slapped her again.

"That is for interrupting." A backhand. "And that is for being wrong."

Juno was almost in shock. No one had *ever* hit her before.

"We do not tolerate mistakes!" Aziz almost spat on her.

She cowered. "What do you want me to do?"

"Find out who this Renquist is."

"How?"

He looked at her with disgust. "Use the gifts that Allah has given you."

The receptionist at Tektel Systems picked up a buzzing line and said, "Tektel Systems."

"Hi, Charlene. It's Helen. Is Harry there?"

"Hold on just a sec, Mrs. Tasker, I'll see."

Helen Tasker stood in her kitchen, absently tasting some homemade icing she was spreading on a birthday cake. The phone was lodged between her shoulder and cheek, so she still had one hand free to swat ineffectually at Dana, who was feeding Gizmo icing on the end of a wooden spoon.

Charlene punched a search on the duty roster; Harry Tasker's name was immediately centered and flagged. Availability code "2."

"He's in a sales meeting, Mrs. Tasker. Let me try and reach him. Hold please."

She punched a key, engaging a digital scrambler. "Line eight, route to 10024."

"Roger, eight to 10024," said a voice in her ear.

In the suite at the Marquis, Gib was reclining on the bed, daydreaming about his eighteenth summer, spent mostly in a hammock on the north shore of the Virgin Islands. . . . His briefcase started ringing.

Gib lunged off the bed and flipped open his case. The cellular scrambler-phone had an LCD screen displaying the following information, "TEKTEL/ CALLER ID POS—TASKER, HELEN."

"It's Helen," said Gib, handing the receiver to Harry.

"Hi, honey," Harry said into the phone, "What's going on?"

Helen was carefully icing the birthday cake, using a round-tipped knife to swirl each stroke into a perfect Betty Crocker peak.

"Sorry to bother you in a meeting, sweetie, but you have to promise me that you'll be home at eight. I don't want Dana and me sitting here by ourselves like we were last year. You promise?"

Harry laughed sheepishly. "Baby, I said I'd be there. Really. Trust me."

The room's phone started ringing.

"Gotta go, honey," said Harry, "I'll see you tonight, okay?"

"Okay. Love you."

"Love you too."

Harry handed the cellular to Gib and accepted the room phone, lifting the receiver.

"Hello? . . . Oh, Juno, hi . . . Well, sure. Uh, I can be there in twenty minutes. Okay, see you then."

Harry hung up and handed the phone to Gib. Gib gave him the fish eye.

"What?" said Harry, grabbing his suit jacket and slipping it on.

"You know what. Goddammit, Harry, if I can't have a happy marriage, then I want to vicariously experience yours. And you're fucking it up for me!"

"Calm down, will you. Her office is on our way home. She says she's got something for me."

"I'm sure she does."

"I'm over it, okay."

"You better be."

He wasn't. From the very first moment he was left alone inside the dim, candlelit Hittite tomb, Harry felt his breath quickening and deepening, and an unwelcome but familiar flutter of anticipation.

Incense burned in wall-mounted censers, giving off an exotic, unidentifiable smell—not at all flowery, but sharp and animal—that seemed to stir the hairs on the back of Harry's neck. Harry looked around. He felt like he was in another age, another world.

A shadow slid across the wall of the entryway behind him. Harry smelled musk mix with the incense and turned.

Juno walked through the door—if what she was doing could properly be called walking. Harry thought that a new word should be coined to signify those sinuous, undulating movements, only a fraction of which were actually involved in propelling her forward.

"Hello, Harry," she said, peering up at him. Her almond-shaped eyes were boldly traced with liner in the ancient Egyptian style. Her hair was scraped away from her high-cheekboned face, and piled high like a crown. And her low-cut evening gown gave new meaning to the word *décolletage*.

Nefertiti, thought Harry, and surely no queen was ever more exquisite.

"Do you like my tomb?" she asked. "The museum financing fell out, so I thought your clients might be interested."

"It's certainly dramatic."

"Especially in this light."

Juno moved closer to Harry. Too close. He could see the perfect glitter of a candle flame in her eyes.

"This is the only light they had then," she said, "so I like to study it this way. I love this place. I love ruins."

"Is that why you got into this business?"

Juno ran her fingers along his lapel, absently smoothing it. "I've always been a collector at heart."

Harry's larynx felt like it was being squeezed in a pair of pliers. He wondered if he spoke, if it would even be intelligible.

She looked up, directly into his eyes. "When I see something I want, I have to have it."

"And you have a reputation as someone who gets what she wants," he rejoined, trying to stay with her. But a croak in his voice ruffled the confident surface of his banter.

Juno's voice was husky, too. "Yes I do."

Harry hoped she hadn't noticed what was painfully clear to him: He was as hard as a *New York Times* crossword puzzle.

An urgent, disembodied, but very real voice reverberated in Harry's skull. "Harry, this is your conscience speaking . . ."

Gib sat in the van, headset firmly in place, parked up the street from Juno's. He had no trouble fleshing out the visuals from the audio he was overhearing. Harry, and many other people Gib held dear, were not safe. Gib to the rescue.

"Snap out of it, baby. Move, move, move!"

"I'd like to see more of the tomb," said Harry. He nodded toward a dimly lit corridor. "What's in there?"

Juno smiled, picked up a candle, and said, "Let's find out."

They walked down the faux-sandstone corridor, lined with bas-reliefs depicting warriors and kings dead for almost three millennia. The flickering candlelight seemed to animate their faces and eyes, bringing them to life.

Juno reached out and caressed the cheek and plaited beard of a warrior chieftain. "Look at him. He died twenty-five centuries ago." Juno pressed her own cheek against the cold stone face, and slowly, gently, ran her nails across the figure.

Harry tried not to think about those nails.

Juno continued: "They breathed and loved and wept, just like us. And now their ideals, their religions, their social orders . . . are gone like mist. What did any of it matter?"

She looked at Harry, and he knew he was in for it now.

"I only hope they lived well," she said.

She began . . . *moving* . . . toward him. She held her head still and level, holding his gaze, but everything underneath was undulating in a variety of circular directions that only accentuated the hypnotic steadiness of her stare.

She stopped well inside his personal space and ran both hands up the broad slope of his chest.

"I only hope they got what they wanted," she whispered. "Because getting what you want is the only important thing."

She kissed him then, very lightly, then left her lips just lying there, infinitely soft, warmly breathing on his mouth.

Gib's spider sense was tingling like a mo'fo'.

"Harry, what's going on?! Listen to the following code word. Helen. H-E-L-E-N. *Do you want me to beep you?*"

* * *

Harry felt his lips mouth the word, "Yes," but no sound came out. He tried again, gasping it out this time, "Yes."

"Oh, yes," said Juno, pressing up against him, enveloping him, mouth opening . . .

Beep! Beep! Beep!

Harry drew down on his beeper quicker than Doc Holliday at the OK Corral. He squinted at the phony number and message displayed, and turned a deeply relieved sigh into a disgusted exhalation.

"It looks like I have to run. I'll call you tomorrow." He took her hand and quickly kissed it. "Your proposal is very interesting."

Harry skedaddled. Juno watched him go, blinking away her amazement.

Gib pumped his fist in the air. "Yes!" he screamed. He checked his watch, looked crestfallen for an instant, then hardened his resolve.

"We can still make it."

Up ahead, he saw Harry turn the corner and walk toward the van.

"Come on, come on, come on!" Gib muttered, starting the van. Harry opened the door and piled in.

Gib pulled away from the curb, asking curiously, "Have you ever heard the phrase, 'Just say no'?"

Harry shook his head, nervously exhausted. "Women. They only want one thing."

Now it was Helen feeding icing to the pea-brained fright wig. She dragged her manicured forefinger through the perfectly sculpted, sugary wavelets, then flopped her arm over the side of the dining chair so

Gizmo could bare his minuscule teeth and flick his tiny rabid tongue all over the baited digit.

The dog tilted his head this way and that, going over the same spot eight times with brainless desperation—any objective person would've taken the horrible little creature outside and fed it to the first *real* dog they saw.

But Helen and Dana were feeling *very subjective* just then. The gayly wrapped presents, the favorite cake, the ice cold favorite dinner—all seemed to mock them, laughing at their pathetic, sappy affection for the undeserving Harry Tasker.

Dana glanced at the clock on the credenza. It was eight-thirty-five.

"See," she said.

Harry was changing his clothes en route, transforming into Harry Tasker, birthday boy. He knew he was late, but maybe not *too* late . . .

Gib snaked through the evening traffic, checking his rearview in that overly attentive way that meant he'd spotted a tail.

"We have a friend," said Gib, bitterly. "Five cars back, inside lane."

Harry, fully changed now, took his seat in the front and checked the sideview mirror.

"Station wagon?"

"Yeah. They've been on us since we left Juno's." Gib shifted down and revved the engine. "I'm gonna lose 'em—"

"Hey! Your turn to think straight. We need this lead."

Gib pounded the steering wheel, knowing it was true.

Harry brought up his rover and spoke into it: "Unit Seven."

Faisil's voice came over the mobile phone. "Seven here."

"I need you at the Georgetown Mall in three minutes."

"Copy that," said Faisil. "We're rolling."

Gib was watching the rearview, but thinking about something else: "Helen's gonna be pissed."

"That's the problem with terrorists," said Harry. "They're really inconsiderate when it comes to people's schedules."

Harry kept his eye on the side mirror. Headlights behind the station wagon momentarily backlit its interior. Three men. Harry guessed the driver was six feet six inches, 275 lbs., maybe a pound of it fat.

"Testing two three," said Harry, shoving a subvocal transceiver into his ear canal.

Gib, headset in place, gave him the thumbs up and pulled the van to the curb in front of the mall.

Half a block away, the station wagon pulled over, too.

Harry slipped on the virtual image Ray-Bans and got out of the car. He paused a moment to light a cigarette from the camera/pack, took a real smoker's drag, and coughed like a twelve-year-old taking his first puff under a bridge.

"You don't smoke, dickhead," said a voice in his ear.

Harry let his hand drop to his side, holding the cigarette pack so that the lens scanned the sidewalk behind him. He walked inside the mall, joining the crowd in the open promenade.

The black-and-white image floated on the left side

of Harry's field of view, perfectly sharp. The two men following him were in plain view. He had been wrong about the driver. He was probably only 260. Vain, thought Harry, spends too much time on the upper body.

But the second guy was worrisome for two reasons. First of all, his full-length coat bulged oddly and considerably on one side. A heavy automatic weapon. Second, he was a runt. He must be an especially mean little cuss to pull this kind of duty. Pin-dick, thought Harry, and he's gonna make America pay.

Gib checked in with his partner. "What's the plan, Stan?"

Harry answered: "Gonna try to get a closer shot of Beavis and Butthead."

"Pick me up a slice while you're in there."

Gib checked the station wagon in his rearview. There was still one man in the backseat. Gib could see the soft cherry glow of his cigarette.

"The other guy's still in the car."

"Stay with him," said Harry.

Gib checked his watch. Keeping his eye peeled on the rearview, he picked up his cellular phone and dialed . . .

"Hi, Helen, it's Gib . . . ." Gib listened to the plaintive protests, then chanted a story as if by rote, as if he'd told it a thousand times before: "Yeah, Harry remembered something he forgot at the office. . . . Yup, we know Harry."

A look of alarm passed over Gib's face as a bus pulled up behind him and filled his rearview mirror. He turned to look out the back windows.

"I will, I promise. We should be there, oh, pretty soon. . . . Okay. 'Bye."

"'Bye," said Helen, and hung up. Dana strode through the room, shoving her arms through the over-sized sleeves of a hockey shirt that served as her jacket.

"Where are you going?" asked Helen.

"Out. If Dad doesn't care enough about us to be here on his birthday, then why should I care? I'm going to a movie."

"No, you're not. You're going to stay here until your father gets home and have cake!"

"Mom, wake up! Dad barely knows we exist!"

Helen felt a resonant pang, hearing the raw hurt beneath her daughter's anger. But as usual, she circled the wagons.

"That's not true, honey—"

"*It is true!*" yelled Dana, silencing her mother. "He doesn't know anything about me, not what counts. He still thinks I'm like ten years old or something. As long as I just smile and say yes to whatever he says, like his good little fantasy daughter, he thinks everything's fine. But it's not fine. Nothing's *fine.*"

Dana stormed out of the kitchen.

"Dana! Come back!" Helen started after her. "Dana—"

The front door slammed.

Gizmo, the reanimated drain clot, pattered over to Helen's feet and gazed up at her. He barked inquiringly.

Helen bent and picked him up, stroking his knobby little head. She pressed her cheek against his silky fur. He licked her face. She hugged him tighter.

Somehow holding him was both a comfort and a door that opened and flooded her with pain.

Harry hung a right at the ham and cheese croissants, and entered a tiled corridor lined with public phones where, for twenty-five cents, you could stand and smell the public restrooms while you talked to a friend.

It was clear to Harry that the men following him were too close, too aggressive to be just tailing him. They didn't seem to care if he saw them or not. They were just waiting for an opportunity to kill him without too many witnesses.

Well, America was the Land of Opportunity. Harry entered the men's room, hoping it would be empty.

Meanwhile, Gib was gnashing his teeth and anthropomorphizing the bus that still blocked his view. He attributed to it all kinds of unflattering human qualities, like an obese rump, an apparently consummated desire for its mother, who was, it seems, a female dog that had given birth to an unintelligent fragment of feces that charged for sex.

The bus finally strained and groaned and polluted its way away from the curb and Gib could see again. The station wagon was empty.

"Oh, shit. Harry, I lost the third guy . . . Harry?"

Gib heard Harry whistling "Edelweiss."

Harry couldn't talk right then. He was apparently taking a leak, looking incongruously stylish with his badass Ray-Bans on.

The runt was standing at the sinks, looking in the mirror, combing uncombable hair. He didn't notice the pack of cigarettes sitting on the counter at the end of the row of sinks.

But Harry didn't even need the virtual image in his sunglasses. He knew how it would play out.

The run's big buddy entered the room and glanced at Harry, who apparently had no idea what was going on behind him.

The big fella and the runt locked eyes in the mirror for an instant, then Mr. Bench Press (who really *was* too proud of his platelike pecs) walked toward the stalls, passing an arm's length behind Harry. He stopped, pointed a silenced Beretta .25 at the back of Harry's skull, and pulled the trigger.

But Harry's head wasn't there. Harry's fist was halfway through the shooter's liver. Harry's other hand was crushing all eight bones in his right wrist. And Harry's palm almost separated his head from his shoulders. The Beretta went flying.

The dimensionally challenged man by the sinks was not idle. He whipped out and leveled his ugly Cobray M-11 with thirty 9mm slugs in its oversized clip.

Harry spun Goliath into an armlock, using him as a human shield.

And then the smaller man made a fatal, though honorable, mistake. He didn't ventilate his partner to get to Harry.

"Yusif! Move!" he cried in Arabic.

But by then Harry had the little man in his sight picture. The Glock went *Crack Crack Crack.*

Harry shot him, and in an odd bit of whimsy, the man's reflection, too.

Yusif took advantage of Harry's divided attention to spin out of the armlock and grab Harry's wrist.

The two of them went careening off the walls, fighting for control of the Glock. They hit a locked stall and popped it open. The big man tripped Harry to the floor, dropping him at the feet of an old gentleman who looked like he'd just crapped a pineapple.

Yusif pounded Harry's gun hand against the door frame, twisted the wrist, and slammed it on his knee. The old guy winced sympathetically. Harry finally cried out and let the gun fall. Yusif reached for it. Harry kicked it to the end of the stalls, then punched Yusif in the face, breaking the big man's nose and knocking him out of the stall. Harry rolled to his feet and went after him. The old man swung the door shut.

Harry lunged toward Yusif, who was turned away, moaning and holding his gushing nose. It was a trap. Harry barely avoided the disemboweling sweep of Yusif's straight razor. Yusif swung forehand, backhand, driving Harry back. Harry suddenly lunged inside the sweep of Yusif's arm, his elbow smashing into the big man's chin. Then Yusif felt a freight train hit him in the balls. He fell to his knees. Harry grabbed him by the forelock and smashed his head repeatedly against a porcelain urinal. When he let go, Yusif sagged to the floor.

Harry pulled a nylon zip strip out of his pocket and handcuffed Yusif's hands behind his back.

Gib was running full out through the promenade, his gut doing the rumba as he dodged annoyed, but respectful pedestrians; Gib had a big automatic in his hand. He pressed one finger to his ear.

"Harry? Harry, you copy?"

Gib felt a wave of relief as he heard, "First-floor restroom, west side."

Harry pulled the groggy, bleeding Yusif to his feet. The door to the restroom banged open. He turned, expecting Gib.

But it was Aziz, with a full-auto Beretta 92-F pointed directly at Harry. And he wasn't sentimental about Yusif. *Bra-a-a-a-a-t.*

Yusif's thickly muscled torso took the full brunt of Aziz's spray. Harry dragged Yusif's deadweight along a few steps, then sprinted for the farthest line of stalls, chased by a steady stream of 9mm slugs that shattered mirrors, exploded porcelain fittings, tore up tiles, and ripped through water pipes. Harry disappeared from view, but Aziz smiled. "Renquist" was trapped.

Aziz strode into the corridor between the stalls. Harry was in one on the left side, so Aziz hosed them all. At nine hundred rounds a minute, it only took a few seconds to put several holes in each.

Aziz let up and listened. No sound. No movement. He walked to the first stall, kicked in the door and sprayed. *Braaaat!* Then the second. Boot, *Brraaat!* The third. Still no Harry. Only three to go. Aziz booted the next door, pulled the trigger—

Out of the corner of his eye, he saw Harry fly out of the end stall, dive to the ground, hydroplane on the flooded floor, and reach for . . .

His Glock. Harry jackknifed into a sitting position and cracked off three rounds before Aziz had time to get a bead. *Crack Crack Crack!* Bullets chased the ducking Aziz out of the stalls, shattering tiles as he sprinted for the door. He got away.

Harry got to his feet and strode inexorably after him.

"Gib, I found the third guy. He's heading back to his car."

"I'm on it."

Harry glanced in at the old gent, still sitting on his throne and in good health, at least physically.

"Sorry about the disturbance, sir," said Harry, and hurried away, past the two bullet-riddled bodies, which lay in a shallow lake filled with glass and tile, past the shattered walls and spraying pipes, past the destroyed urinals and splintered mirrors.

Interior by Harry.

Aziz hurtled onto the sidewalk in front of the mall and ran toward the station wagon, his giant machine-pistol and wild eyes creating quite a stir.

Gib ran out of the mall a second later.

"Freeze!" he yelled, leveling his pistol. Mistake. Too many pedestrians.

And Aziz didn't care. *Brraaaaat!* People screamed and scattered as Gib ran behind a light pole not quite wide enough to protect both his ass and his beer gut. A hail of slugs clanged off the pole as Gib vacillated. He decided to sacrifice his ass for the greater good, closed his eyes and gingerly stuck it out. A slug tore out his wallet, and he instinctively pulled in, exposing his belly—a slug opened his shirt, another sliced his tie in half. Gib realized this was a poor choice of cover.

"Wrong! This is not good!"

But Aziz suddenly turned and ran. Gib couldn't believe his luck. He kissed the pole.

"Harry, where are you?" said Gib, warily tailing Aziz.

"Be there in a second," came the answer.

Aziz sprinted for his car, knocking over pedestrians, checking behind him. He was almost to his goal when a large man hurtled through one of the mall's decorative windows, hit the sidewalk, and rolled up in a shooting crouch, holding a Glock pointed directly at his face.

Aziz dodged toward the street, slung a young woman into Harry's line of fire, and ran into traffic.

"Get down!" yelled Harry, itching to empty his clip into Aziz. But now there were drivers in cars to worry about.

Heedless of the braking, honking cars, Aziz sprinted across the street, leaping and sliding off the hood of a car that couldn't stop in time. He made it across, then glanced back.

Harry was steaming toward him like a battleship, making a beeline, jumping over the stalled cars.

Aziz whirled around, looking for a way out. Allah was merciful.

A young biker on a nimble little Kawasaki 250 threaded his way through the jam at the intersection. Aziz sprinted for him, clotheslining the kid just as he started to accelerate away. Seconds later, Aziz straddled the bike and popped the clutch. He cut across the road and headed for the park.

Harry was running flat out. He saw Aziz's new tack and cut across on a diagonal, taking an angle he hoped would give him a decent shot.

Aziz raced onto a bike path that circled a lake. He opened his throttle wide. He saw Harry taking the angle, but smiled, knowing Harry would be too late.

Harry knew it, too, though neither despair nor helplessness attended this realization. He scanned his surroundings, never slowing, saw the mounted Metro policeman, and darted toward him.

The mounted cop enjoyed his job. He kind of felt powerful up there, like John Wayne— An astonishingly strong grip closed around his arm and pulled him off his horse. He tasted grass.

"Federal officer in pursuit of a suspect," said Harry, mounting up. "Sorry." Harry clicked his tongue and spurred the beast and he was gone.

"Hey!" The cop fumbled for his sidearm, but he wasn't the fastest draw in the West.

Aziz tore along the bike path, terrorizing joggers and those ridiculous Western power walkers. Bicyclists swerved into benches and trees, their delicate ten-speeds twisting into pretzels. Aziz tossed a glance over his shoulder. Just routine. He did a pretty comic double take for a terrorist.

A large man holding a Glock was galloping along a tree-lined ridge, closing in on Aziz's flank.

Aziz growled, then said something like "spawn of a lizard turd!" and tore off the path onto the grass. Like Harry, Aziz was not one to append feelings of helplessness and despair to an unfortunate turn of events. He decided to turn the chase into a steeplechase.

They hurtled into a stand of trees, scattering lovers and drug addicts.

Aziz readied his gun in his left hand, planning to catch Harry off guard at the moment he came out of the trees.

Aziz sped into the open, stood on his foot pegs and turned to fire.

Harry was way ahead of him. The Glock was spitting suppression fire as soon as he galloped out of the trees.

Aziz's aim was spoiled as he ducked and took evasive action. He fired blindly behind him, and suddenly his gun was empty.

Aziz cursed and flung the gun high in the air, hoping to bean Harry with it. He cut to his right, twisted every inch out of his throttle, and shot back toward the edge of the park.

Gib fought the wheel of the van, honking and screaming for the right-of-way. He brought up his mike.

"Harry, what's your twenty?"

"Westbound in the park," Harry said calmly. He and his horse were clattering over slippery cobblestones, chasing Aziz around a big fountain. Panicked ducks flapped and quacked annoyingly, begging for Harry to shoot them.

Aziz came out of his turn and took off toward the street.

Harry spurred his horse back to a gallop. "Suspect is on a Kawa 250. He's going to come out on Franklin. Hold on a second . . ." Harry paused to concentrate on jumping a park bench, then continued. "I want you over on Fourteenth in case he turns south. And I need Unit Seven on the north side to box him in."

Gib made a quick turn, obeying his orders. "Copy that."

"And make it fast," said Harry. "My horse is getting tired."

Gib blinked. *"Your horse? . . ."*

* * *

Aziz exploded out of the bushes that lined the park. Cars braked and skidded out of control, bashing into each other. He turned south and wove through the confusion.

Harry and his horse took the hedgerow in one big stride. They came down amidst a crush of stalled cars. Harry gathered the reins, looked around, and spotted the motorcycle. Hi-yo Silver and away. Harry jumped the hood of a crashed car, hot on Aziz's trail.

Aziz turned the wrong way onto a one-way street, speeding down the empty left-turn lane. But a familiar white van swerved toward him, accelerating, sliding broadside. . . .

Aziz braked and swung broadside, too, stopping inches from the side of the van. Aziz looked to his left. "Renquist" was galloping around the corner. To his right, the one with no wallet was running around from the far side of the van. There was only one way out.

Up those red-carpeted stairs into the Georgetown Park Hotel. Aziz popped the clutch and wheelied across the road, dropping his wheel onto the sidewalk and trail-riding up the stairs.

Hotel staff and guests scattered as the bike roared toward them. The doorman reflexively opened the glass door. Aziz shot inside.

The guests uttered cries of shock and horror, at least until they saw the guy on the horse clatter up the stairs. Then they shut up.

The doorman stared.

"Open the door stupid." Harry raised his Glock. "What, you want a tip?"

The doorman opened the door. Harry bent low and spurred his horse toward the reception desk.

Acres of quiet marble and burgundy carpet. Muted elegance: That's what the brochure said, describing both its decor and clientele.

Vrrrrrooooooom! Aziz knocked Mr. Lincoln Town Car on his ass, leaving his satiny, bejeweled mistress with her mouth agape and standing in a cloud of motorcycle exhaust.

" 'Scuse me, ma'am," said Harry, as his horse leapt the couch next to her.

Aziz slid and weaved his way down a narrow, crowded service corridor. Room service trolleys, maid's service trolleys, mobile clothing racks with spotless dry-cleaning, few of these survived his passage, and those that did went down under Trigger's thundering hoofs and heaving flanks.

Aziz burst through some swinging doors into the hotel kitchen, running down cooks, ruining soufflés. He looked behind him.

Harry and his horse were right there, picking their way through his chaotic wake.

Aziz was beginning to seriously resent Harry. He twisted the throttle wide open and the bike leapt forward, heading for the doors to the hotel restaurant.

It was the kind of place that served entrees so spartan that normal people took one look at them and bust out laughing. But this wasn't a place for the rabble. This was a restaurant for people who enjoyed excruciating pangs of hunger, who reveled in the long wait between skimpy courses that did nothing to alleviate their agony. This was a restaurant for refined masochists. And tonight was going to be their night.

Vrrrrrooooom! Aziz burst through the doors and

upended two tables and four guests in the first seconds. A man started screaming, mistaking an authentic marinara for his own blood.

Harry burst through next, his gelding stamping and sweating and foaming, hooves splintering a table, splattering fresh brioche.

Harry quickly zeroed in on the only motorcycle in the joint, raised his gun beside his face, and gave his horse the heel.

Aziz saw Harry bearing down. He leaned the bike way over, propping it with his leg as he skidded in a tight turn around a marble fountain.

Mr. Tax Evader, seated on the fountain's edge, yanked up his legs and fell into the drink.

Aziz pulled out of his turn and roared toward a party of six.

Mr. Tax Evader climbed out of the fountain, upset about the condition of his tux. Trigger galloped by, insisting he wash it again.

Now about that party of six. Aziz was clearly considering riding over them. Their mouths opened. They started to stand. Aziz decided he wouldn't get through after all, and spun broadside just as they started screaming in panic.

The fleeing patrons tipped the table toward Aziz, emptying several dinners under his back wheel. He popped his clutch, trying to pull away, but the wheel spun in the goo, unable to get traction, and incidentally creating several new taste sensations and distributing them around the room to the guests.

Harry saw Aziz hung up in a puddle of slop. He spurred his horse, bringing the Glock to bear, ready to shoot Aziz dead and then ride him down.

But Aziz's wheel cleared a crepe—flinging it across

the room onto Mr. Thurston Howell III's face—and Aziz was off to the races again.

Harry and Trigger crashed into the upended table. The horse stumbled, its legs tangled dangerously in a chair.

Aziz sped through the restaurant's main doors, into the lobby.

Two glass elevators serviced the guests, set side by side in a gleaming transparent tower inside a lobby whose ceiling was the roof itself, twenty stories away.

Aziz would never have noticed the elevators except that just ahead, barricaded behind a pile of lobby furniture, Gib and Faisil were peering at him down the barrels of their handguns.

All of a sudden, the elevator door that opened took on an urgent allure, literally obsessional in its intensity. Aziz braked, skid, throttled up, all in one motion, shooting forward into the elevator, which was occupied by a very shocked and frightened young woman.

Gib and Faisil ran out and covered the elevator, but by then Aziz had the woman around the neck, a knife at her throat.

"Stay where you are!" ordered Aziz, punching the top floor's button with the tip of his knife.

"Let her go!" screamed Gib, wasting breath.

Aziz sneered, waiting patiently. The doors closed and Aziz sailed upward in plain sight of everyone below.

Gib hit the call button for the other elevator: it was almost down anyway, bringing an elderly couple to the lobby.

Harry cantered up to Gib and Faisil, his eyes following theirs, assessing the situation. The second elevator opened and Harry walked his horse in, trapping the old couple at the back of the car.

"Watch the exits," he said to Gib and Faisil, then turned to the old man. "Would you press the top floor please?"

"Certainly," said the man, leaning sideways to obey. The doors closed and they started up. The horse twirled around trying to get comfortable. The man and his wife ended up in the worst possible position: nose to tail.

They'd been to a lot of parades. They knew what was going to happen. The woman began to weep.

Harry, meanwhile, had two blue, implacably cold eyes locked on Aziz, who was two floors above him over in the next shaft.

And Aziz likewise had his eyes on Harry. The "Renquist" pig was locked on him like a smart missile. Aziz had never been so enraged in his life. He had never hated *anyone* so much in his life. It was making him unconsciously choke his hostage. She scratched at his arm, croaking, and he let up a bit. He tried to think of a plan, but none came. Once on the roof, he'd have nowhere to go. And there was nothing but death in those blue eyes below.

Harry, too, smelled blood. He put a fresh clip into his Glock, absently handing the old clip to the elderly woman.

She took it with a trembling hand, then turned back to stare into the crack of doom. She glanced up at the floor number. Eighteen! Almost there. Oh please, God. Oh, please—Oh, God! The horse's tail was slowly lifting. Her heart stopped. The horse-apples would start rolling any second. She filled her lungs to scream—but Trigger only swished his tail across her face.

Aziz's elevator door opened onto the roof, and he roared out onto the deck, speeding to the edge, stopping at the low glass barrier. No way out. Unless . . . Aziz turned around and sped back toward the center of the roof.

His terrified hostage was disappearing back down through the roof. Harry's elevator arrived. Aziz brodied the bike into a one-eighty.

Harry's elevator opened and Harry rode out with his Glock pointed in front of him.

And Aziz took off for the edge of the roof. He didn't stop. He smashed through the glass barrier and launched into space.

Harry rode to the edge in time to see Aziz clear a sixty-foot jump and splash into the rooftop pool of a fifteen-story building next door.

Harry couldn't believe it. He was getting away! Harry wheeled his horse, took him back to the elevators, wheeled him again.

"Haaah! Haaah!" yelled Harry, spurring him, grabbing his mane low down, giving him his head. The horse shot forward, thundered across the roof, accelerating, going full tilt.

But a horse is not a motorcycle. It has a brain. Trigger slammed his front hooves down and Harry went flying over the horse's head and over the edge of the roof. Luckily he still had hold of the reins. *Smash!* Harry kissed the glowing red Marriott sign. That hurt. He hung there, shaking his head clear. He looked behind and below. Damn!

The creep was climbing out of the pool and getting away.

Harry looked up at his horse. Its head was bent low between locked, widely splayed forelegs.

"Back up, boy! Come on, you can do it! Back up! I'm not mad! I swear!"

The horse hesitated, then did what it was told. Harry slid upward onto the roof and climbed to his feet, panting. He turned and looked at his horse.

"What the hell were you thinking? We had the guy and you let him get away!"

The horse's big brown eyes showed hurt: Harry lied; he *was* mad.

"What kind of cop are you? Glue factory, tomorrow morning, ten A.M. I'm going to render you myself."

A hard fall rain slapped at the street as Gib dropped Harry off. Harry hurried to the front door, hopeful: There was a light on in the dining room.

But in fact, Helen was asleep at the dining-room table, head on her arms, beside a bowl of melted vanilla ice cream.

Harry padded in silently, stopped at the end of the table, and looked at her. So sad. He felt an unfamiliar emotion and tried to identify it. He was sorry, that was one part of it; and hurt that he had hurt Helen and Dana, that was another; but he was also angry. For the first time in his life, Harry realized he resented his job. That shocked him. It was without question a job that had to be done. And without question, he was indispensable. But something about his situation had changed, not so much inside him, or with the job, but with his wife and daughter. He felt as if he'd pushed them both to some kind of edge, like they were on the cusp of something. . . . With a nauseating feeling of terror, terror that he never felt in a merely life-threatening situation, he realized he was in danger of losing them. They needed him *now*.

A dishrag stirred next to Helen's arm, sniffed a couple of times, and coughed. Then it stood, drawing itself up to its full height of four inches, and barked a friendly hello.

Harry walked over and gave the dog a pat. Helen lifted her sleepy head.

"I'm so sorry, honey. I raced home as quick as I could. I really wanted—"

Helen stretched. "Mmmm—It's okay, don't bother, Harry."

He bent and kissed her hair, then bent her head back and kissed her on each eye. He pulled away, looking straight into her slightly surprised eyes.

"I'm sorry. Thank you for the party."

"Yeah. It was fun, right Gizmo?"

Helen smiled up at Harry, and Harry felt a little of the weight lift from his chest. Maybe things weren't so bad as he thought. He was just tired.

Helen stood and sighed, running her hands over her husband's broad chest.

Harry put his around her. "You want me to open my presents?"

Helen shook her head. "Let's go to bed. There's only one present you have to open tonight."

"Oh . . . I get it," he said, slowly nodding.

Helen giggled and pulled him along toward the bedroom.

Harry fell backward onto the bed, pushed there by his one-track-minded wife.

"Don't move," she said, "I'll be right back."

She hit the play button on the CD. Kenny G. Saxual healing. Helen gave Harry a final warning look and disappeared into the bathroom.

"Hey, where you going? Come on to bed."

Helen opened a cupboard and pulled out an iced bucket of champagne and two glasses.

"I'll just be a second," she yelled. She reached into a shopping bag and pulled out a handful of brand new lingerie, separating and identifying the unfamiliar items. Oh my God. Look at those G-string panties. Suddenly, all her boldness drained away. What if this was a big mistake? She'd asked Harry about lingerie before, whether he liked it, and he always said he didn't need that stuff. Allison said that's what most men say, like they don't want you to think they can't pop a boner at will. But watch them with a Victoria's Secret catalogue when they don't know you're looking. Or wear some lingerie without asking: They start barking and turn into Vlad the Impaler.

Helen recovered her courage and determination. "So what happened tonight at the office?" she called out, putting on her very pretty, and very sheer lace bra.

Harry sighed. "I couldn't believe it. I got back to get this report I need, right, and the phone is ringing, so like a bonehead I answer it . . ."

Helen hurriedly slipped on her outrageous panties, then sheer black stockings.

Harry continued lying, so practiced he needed only a small part of his brain for the job: "It's this big client in Japan." He yawned hugely, talking through the yawn: "And it's the middle of the morning there and their whole system is crashed . . . The guy's having a meltdown . . ."

Helen heard him pause. "Wha'd you do, honey?" she asked, trying to figure out which way her garter belt goes.

"Well, I pull out the manual on their setup, which is the new 680 server I told you about . . ."

Helen fastened the garters to the tops of the stockings.

". . . And I'm troubleshooting it with them over the phone . . . talking to a translator, right, who's getting half of it wrong . . . it was unbelievable . . . really wild."

Helen stepped into black stiletto heels. "It sounds wild," she said, opening and applying her lipstick in a single smooth motion. "So now you're the big hero, right? For fixing their system?"

"Uh-huh."

"My husband the hero." Helen applied a touch of cologne here and, yes, there, and looked at herself in the mirror.

She looked nasty. And she looked good. And surprise, surprise, the lingerie was turning *her* on.

Helen poured two glasses of champagne, doubting they'd have time to drink it.

"Here I come, honey, just a second." She put down the bottle, picked up the glasses . . .

And strode into the bedroom like a living 900 number.

Harry made a noise something like "Ghkkhonkskxonk!" It wasn't a mating call.

Helen stared down at her snoring husband, her shoulders slumping in shock. She sat down on the bed, staring into space, then noticed the champagne glasses in her hand. She tipped one back, draining it.

"Happy Birthday, Harry," she said without turning around.

Four

Gib gazed at his partner with speculative concern. Harry had his game face on, which was fine if you were engaged in an antiterrorist operation. But for staking out your kid's high school, trying to catch her playing hookey? Gib shook his head; I don't think so.

Harry scanned the campus, peering through gigantic binoculars. "Why don't they tie their fucking shoes?" he wondered aloud. . . . Baggy pants, baggy shirts, mushroom haircuts. "Jesus. It's a clown college."

Gib sighed. He picked up the cellular phone, pretending to call the office.

"Hey, did that guy Harry chased last night turn himself in yet? 'Cause apparently that's the only way we're going to catch the son of a bitch."

Harry wasn't even listening. "Okay. Here she comes."

Dana skipped down the front stairs of the school

and walked to the curb, waving at—Harry panned the binoculars—Trent! He knew it!

The little shit rocketed up on his motorcycle. Dana got on, adjusted her Walkman's headphones, and Trent launched into the road, weaving through the light traffic.

Harry pulled out, hurrying to keep pace.

"Look at the way the little punk is driving. He's all over the place!" He glanced at Gib for support. "He hasn't signaled once!"

Goddammit, that's outrageous." Gib wrestled his gun out and cocked it. "I'll teach that little puke not to signal! Come on, Harry! Give me a shot!"

Gib was not being supportive. Harry concentrated on cutting off a car full of kids who foolishly thought Harry would stop at the big red octagon. Harry sped through the intersection, his mind focused on Trent . . . Yes, his would be a lingering death.

Dana heard angry honking behind her and twisted around to look. Hey, that was . . . that was her *father* driving that van.

"Oh, my God! I think that's my dad!"

Trent checked his rearview and gave a snort of mixed hilarity and disgust. So the old fart was tailing them. That's how he showed interest in his daughter.

"Hang on!" Trent yelled, and downshifted. He shot forward, slaloming between cars, getting ahead of the pack and sliding left.

"So you wanna play, huh?" Harry downshifted, too. He darted expertly into the middle lane, then slid into the turnout, following Trent into the left turn the motorcycle was obviously braking for.

Except at the last second Trent opened the throttle

and cut sharply right, in front of the honking cars heading straight. Harry slammed on his brakes, coming to a stop in the middle of the intersection, stranded there as a stream of cars passed him on both sides.

Trent's rice burner roared away, beeping its horn twice, like the Roadrunner goosing the Coyote.

Gib exploded with laughter. "Ha! The little prick ditched you! That is so goddam funny!"

"Son of a bitch!" Harry yelled.

"Can we go to the office now, Mr. Superspy?"

Harry sat at his workstation in Omega Sector, electronically flipping through headshots of known terrorists. Gib and Faisil sat on either side of him, looking drained; after an hour of *Click Click Click* and a thousand ugly faces they were ready to drink hemlock.

But Harry still had the same blank focused look he'd started with. *Click Click.* All of a sudden his eyes narrowed. His finger hovered over the mouse button.

Gib and Faisil perked up.

A heavily bearded man with a full head of wiry hair stared out at them. Harry put his hands on the screen, framing out everything but the man's eyes.

Gib and Faisil saw it, too.

You can grow hair or lose it, sculpt bones and inject lipids, tuck skin and even change its color. But you can't change the look in a person's eyes.

Trilby perused the hardcopy photo and file of Aziz.

"Salim Abu Aziz," said Harry. "Syrian national. Hardcore, highly fanatical, ultrafundamentalist."

"Linked to numerous car-bombings," added Gib, "The '89 cafe bomb in Rome was his, and the 727 out of Lisbon last year. Major player."

"Now he's formed his own splinter faction called Crimson Jihad," said Faisil.

Gib nodded. "Guess the other terrorist groups were too warm and fuzzy for his taste."

"They call him the Sand Spider," said Faisil.

"Why?" asked Trilby.

Faisil had done some research: "Probably because it sounds scary."

Harry summed it up. "He's our man. All the evidence is circumstantial, but there's just too much to ignore."

Trilby, far from pleased, eyed Harry with the intimidating stare he usually reserved for junior agents.

Harry realized he must've really pissed him off with the Wild West show.

Which he had. Trilby's mildest response to a public donnybrook like yesterday's was six months exile to Data Input. But Trilby couldn't afford to lose Harry right now. He *had* to cut Harry some slack, and that really made his prostate swell. Slack in itself was an odious concept, but to be helplessly *forced* into it, instead of dispensing it at his pleasure—well, he was going to remember this, and that's what he was telling Harry with his glittering blue eye.

"This *is* impressive, gentlemen . . ."

Uh-oh. The old man said something nice.

". . . Of course, it would be even more impressive if you *actually knew where he was*."

"We'll get him," said Harry.

"Yes, you will," rejoined Trilby, with drawled menace.

Harry nodded to his comrades and they stood to go. Trilby waited till they relaxed, till they really thought they'd gotten away.

"About last night . . ."

Three sphincters tightened as one. Three minds screamed the identical obscenity.

Trilby pulled a newspaper off the counter behind him and tossed it in front of Harry. The photo was in color; right beside a headline that said "Man Attacks Motorcyclist! Destroys Mall, Hotel!" The photo showed a man, mostly obscured by a hand thrust right up to the camera lens, leading a horse out of a glass elevator.

"I prefer my agents to stay off the front page," said Trilby in an evil whisper.

"What could I do sir? He ran away before I could smash his camera."

Trilby's eye blazed. "I'll be sure to repeat your little joke to the President when I brief him today. Right after he tears me a new asshole." Trilby stared Harry down. "We're in the middle of a national emergency, but even so, I'm going to pencil in an hour every day for me to daydream about how I'm going to revenge myself on you three. When this is over, I am going to make you squeal. Count on it."

Trilby watched them go, knowing they would believe him, even though he'd been lying through his teeth. In an agency full of professional liars, he was the most accomplished of them all.

It's just that he wanted Harry on thin ice. Because that's what Trilby saw stretching in every direction.

* * *

"**H**ey, what're you doing?" said Gib as Harry pulled
the van over, across the street from Helen's office
building.

Harry handed him the keys. "Look, uh . . . I've
got to talk to Helen about this thing with Dana. I'm
just going to run in and see if she can get away for
lunch. Hang here for a while, will you?"

Gib was pleasantly astonished; Harry was willingly
seeking out the company of a family member during
his work day. On the other hand, that meant Gib
would be sitting in the van for an hour, further
inflaming his hemorrhoids. Not too thrilling.

"You want me to hang, like, *through lunch*?"

"Yeah. Hang," said Harry getting out.

Gib moved over into the driver's seat, eyeing Harry
bitterly. "I'll just hang then, shall I?" he said, reaching for the cellular phone. Harry walked away. Gib
punched one of the memory buttons, and waited.

"Yeah, large cheese pizza, thin crust, and a Diet
Coke . . . delivery."

Harry walked into Kettleman Barnes and smiled at
the receptionist with a cordiality he did not sincerely
feel. In a perverse parallel to the process of evolution,
law firms had, for generations, unnaturally selected
receptionists for the irritating quality of their voices.
So successful were they, that now, in modern times,
the artificial nasality, mixed with a sadistic, robotic
musicality, had reached such a pitch of refinement
that the receptionists could almost *see* their callers
squirming on the other end of the line.

It kept them bright and cheery through the long
day.

"Hellooo, Mr. Ta-*sker*. A-one moment, pleeease—"

She punched a button, talking into her headset. "Kettleman Baaaarnes. A-one moment pleeeease. . . . I'll buzz Mrs. Tasker for you now, Mr. Ta-*sker*."

Harry felt his gun arm twitch. The Glock was right there, the clip full . . .

"Uhm, no, no I'd like to surprise her," Harry said. "Thanks, I know where her desk is."

Harry made his way down a narrow aisle between tiny, cramped offices carved out of the communal space with fabric-covered partitions. The cubicle/offices overflowed with papers, and files, and hard-working paralegals.

Harry neared his wife's cubicle. He heard a phone ring ahead, heard Allison's voice say, "Helen Tasker's office."

Harry was about to come into view, when Allison said, "Helen! It's your Mystery Man."

"Simon?" gasped Helen, "Ohmigod."

Harry stopped in his tracks. Simon?

"Go go go!" he heard Helen say. Harry quickly turned into a vacant cubicle as Allison crossed the aisle to her own desk.

Helen spoke quietly into the phone. "Hello, Simon? . . . Yes, I can talk. There's no one around . . . You mean right now? . . . I guess I could . . . Okay, I'll be right there."

Helen sounded nervous, guilty, and *excited*. And Harry heard it all. His face flushed red; his breath was coming in shallow gasps. He desperately tried to put this together in some way that didn't spell C-U-C-K-O-L-D.

But seconds later, all hope was lost, his whole world was shattered, and Harry Tasker was in ruins.

"Yes, yes," she said breathlessly, with muted passion, "I can't wait. . . . 'Bye."

A roar filled Harry's head and the edges of his vision went gray. He staggered a little.

Helen's voice: "Can you cover me for an hour?"

"Just an hour?" said Allison. "You should tell this stud to take more time."

"Will you shut up," said Helen, packing her purse, "I should never have told you about him."

Helen hurried down the aisle. She didn't even notice the big man bent over the desk in the next cubicle.

Gib sat in the van, kind of happy, actually. He had a soft pillow under him, a pizza on the way, and there were a ton of women pouring onto the street, heading for their favorite lunch spots.

And then he saw Harry staggering into the road like a zombie, looking neither right nor left, holding his gut.

Jesus, he's been shot, thought Gib, opening his door and running into the street.

Harry was oblivious to the cars, the taxi, the bus—*Screeech! Honk!* Gib ran to his side and dragged him quickly away toward the van.

"What happened?" He pulled Harry's hands away from his stomach. No holes. "You look like you got gut-kicked. What's the matter? You sick?"

Harry leaned against the van for support.

Gib was as near as he would ever get to panic; he'd *never* seen Harry like this.

He . . . Helen," stammered Harry. "It's Helen. It's Helen, Gib."

"Something to do with Helen is what I'm getting," said Gib.

"She's having an affair!" Harry's face pleaded with Gib to save him, to tell him it wasn't true, to do something to relieve the awful agony in his gut.

Gib gaped. Then broke into a big grin. "Congratulations!" he yelled, hugging his buddy. "Welcome to the club."

"It can't be," Harry said, slumping against the car. "Not Helen."

"Yup. Same thing happened to me with wife two," Gib said, with a "been there, done that" casualness. "Except I had no idea until I came home and the house was empty. I mean empty. She even took the ice-cube trays from the fridge. What kind of a sick person would think of that?"

"I still don't believe it!" wailed Harry.

"Relax. Helen still loves you. She just wants this guy to bang her." That got Harry's attention. "It's nothing serious. You'll get used to it after a—"

Harry lifted Gib by the lapels and slammed him against the van.

"Stop cheering me up!"

Gib didn't bat an eye. But he stopped being flip. He looked into his friend's angry, tortured face and said, almost sleepily, "What did you expect, Harry? She's a flesh-and-blood woman. And you're never there. It was only a matter of time."

The pain in Harry's face only deepened. But Gib was right. It was all his fault. Harry let go of Gib's jacket.

"Let's concentrate on work," said Gib, opening the door for Harry. "That's how I always got through it when my life turned to dog shit. We'll catch some terrorists and beat the shit out of them. You'll feel a whole lot better."

Harry climbed in the van and closed the door. What do I *do*? he thought.

Gib got in and started the van. "Women," he said, "can't live with 'em. Can't kill 'em." He pulled out into traffic.

No, thought Harry, this wasn't *women*. This was Helen. And Harry realized with total resignation that he couldn't imagine life without her.

Gib was wrong. He wouldn't drown his sorrows in work; he wouldn't take out his frustrations on a terrorist's head. Well, maybe he would, but it wouldn't make him feel better. No. He had a problem, and he was going to *attack* it.

The Listening Room at Omega Sector was a very hushed sort of place: an entire wall of silent DAT recorders turned slowly, recording phone calls, e-mail, faxes, Teletypes, banking transactions, even television transmissions siphoned off by spy satellites thousands of miles away.

Along another wall, a row of technicians in sound-proof cubicles processed and collated transcripts spat out by high-speed laser printers.

Harry and Gib walked along a Lexan wall separating them from the bank of DAT recorders.

"'The Chief's given us a blank check on wiretaps," Gib said, "so I've set 'em up on all of Juno's shipping agents, her clients, and Faisil made up a list of possible contacts that Crimson Jihad might have in this country. Now all we can do is wait—"

Gib noticed Harry was staring at the recorders, as if mesmerized by the slowly turning spools.

"Is this national security stuff boring you?"

"Put a tap on her phone," grunted Harry.

"What're you talking about? We have that."

"*Helen's* phone. Her office line and the line at my house."

Gib stared openmouthed at Harry.

Harry's jaw was set, his eyes dead serious.

Gib glanced around nervously. "Okay, I have two words to describe that idea. In. Sane. Unauthorized wiretap is a felony, pard."

Harry grabbed Gib and rammed him up against the Lexan wall. "We do it twenty times a day! Don't give me that crap. Just put in the tapes. *Now!*"

"Sure, Harry. I'm on it," said Gib, nodding reassuringly, as if to a nutball.

Harry let him go, staring down a curious techie watching from a transcript cubicle.

Gib straightened his jacket and shook his head. The big guy was losing it. "Seek help, Harry," he said, and headed for the door of the Listening Room.

Harry walked off toward his workstation, projecting the delicate aura of a bulldozer. He was an irresistible force, and there was no such thing as an immovable object. That had always been his way.

But even Harry wondered how he could be so absolutely certain that the tap on Helen's phone was as urgent, if not more urgent, than the one on Juno Skinner's. Gib thought Harry was becoming irrational. But from where Harry stood, it made perfect sense.

Helen and Dana, preparing dinner in the kitchen, looked puzzled as they heard the front door being unlocked. Who could that be—? They heard Harry bellow, "I don't smell any fooood!"

Helen and Dana looked at each other, and then at the kitchen clock. It wasn't even six o'clock. They hadn't even started cooking. Harry walked into the kitchen.

"What's going on in here?" he said with mock disapproval, giving them each a kiss. "You need somebody to get things going?"

"I just got home," protested Helen, still in shock.

"I'm going to wash up," said Harry, "and then I'm going to make some potatoes."

Helen and Dana watched him go, wondering what was up.

Helen was pleasantly surprised, though guilty about how she'd spent her lunch hour.

Dana's expectations, however, were pretty pessimistic. First he tails her, then he comes home early. Nothing good could come of this.

Dinnertime was full of awkward silences. Helen and Harry smiled at each other once or twice and snickered shyly, both pretending it was the novelty of the situation that made them tongue-tied. Lies piled on lies. The whole thing was truly amazing to Harry.

He'd been acting for seventeen years. But knowing his wife and daughter were doing the same thing somehow just blew him away. The web of lies and guilty secrets these three people were enmeshed in was absolutely astonishing.

Harry decided to probe. He wanted to *see* them lie, wondering if they could do it properly. He swallowed a mouthful of buttery mashed potatoes and eyed his daughter.

"How was school today?"

"Fine," she said with sunny finality. She would have passed a polygraph.

Harry ate some more potatoes, then looked at his wife.

"I came by to see you today. To have lunch. But you were gone."

"You did?" Helen panicked an instant, Harry could see that, but smothered it quickly. "You must have just missed me."

"They said you had to run out."

"Yeah. It was a rush thing. They needed some documents down at the courthouse."

"Oh."

Helen warmed to her subject. "Our printer was out. So I had to go downstairs and use their printer, and when I got there, my documents weren't formated for their computer—It was crazy. I barely made it."

Harry nodded. Quite a performance. "So a little excitement in an otherwise dull day," he said. "Did it work out okay?"

"Oh, sure. Fine." Helen got up. "I'll get some more gravy."

Dana watched them. Her dad was acting really weird and quiet. Her mom was nervous. Yuck! She didn't want to know!

"I'm done," she said, and bolted from the table, leaving behind a full plate of artfully rearranged food.

Harry found himself alone, poking at a pile of green beans. What a mess.

But he had to be patient. This was an op. First you surveill. Gather intelligence. And above all, you keep your cool.

Five

Harry plowed out of the Listening Room, a vein as blue and thick as the Danube bulging in his forehead. A sheaf of transcripts, pleated and crushed like a giant white bow tie, was clamped in one giant paw.

Gib, seated at his workstation, saw Harry coming and commended his spirit unto God.

"Where's page ten?" thundered Harry.

"What do you mean?" said Gib, backing away, looking totally innocent.

"Don't bullshit me. These transcripts. They jump from page nine to eleven. Give it to me."

Gib sagged. "Harry, I'm your friend—"

"Now!"

Gib reached into his back pocket and pulled out a folded sheet of paper. Harry snatched it and read, his eyes bulging.

Underneath the date, time, and project authorization code, the conversants were designated simply as Male and Female.

F: Hello?

M: Helen? It's Simon.

F: Yes. Go ahead.

M: I can't talk long now. Can you meet me for lunch tomorrow? I must see you.

F: Yes, I suppose so.

M: The same place. One o'clock. I have to go now. See you tomorrow. Remember I need you.

Harry smashed the paper into a ball.

"Blood pressure, Harry."

Helen, reading on her exercise bike, glanced up as Harry came into the bedroom.

"Hi," she said, giving him a quick smile.

Too quick. "I thought we might have lunch tomorrow," Harry said.

"Oh . . . I can't, honey. I promised Allison I'd go shopping with her. Sorry." The smile again.

"No problem," he said, levelly.

Helen struggled to concentrate on her book, eyes and thoughts rebeling.

Surreal, thought Harry. This was *Helen* smoothly lying to him. Harry walked behind her, lifted her purse off a chair, and walked into the hall.

Gib stood outside Harry's bathroom window, shoulders hunched against a cold rain. The window slid up and a purse sailed out. He caught it.

Harry leaned out the window. "Ten minutes," he whispered, and disappeared.

Gib hurried off with the purse.

"I'm taking the rat for a walk," yelled Harry,

turned up his collar, and walked out the front door with Gizmo on a leash.

Gib's van was parked a little ways down the rainy street. Harry strode quickly toward it. Gizmo, as was his wont, stopped to check his messages, and suddenly found himself arcing through the air and landing three feet from where he'd stopped. He moved his little legs rapidly, keeping up for a moment. But eventually his gigantic brain wandered and he slowed, looking around for a butt to sniff. Whoopa! He was sailing through the air again.

Harry walked under a dripping maple overhanging the road and opened the door of the van.

Inside, in a pool of warm light, Gib was bent over the base of Helen's purse, wielding a jeweler's screwdriver.

A great wave of Gib-smell washed over Gizmo, causing all twelve of his neurons to fire in panic. *Rowf, rowf!*

Gib spun around and growled, then projected a big "Woof!"

Gizmo scampered behind Harry's legs.

"You know what, Harry?" said Gib, stitching the purse's leather back up, "I think you're going about this whole thing all wrong. See women, they like you to talk to them. You know? And maybe the problem is you're not in touch with your feminine side." Gib snipped the excess thread and looked up at Harry. "You know I was watching Sally Jesse Raphael—"

Harry held up one finger. On Harry's forehead, the Danube was in full flood.

Gib realized Harry was about to drive that finger deep into one of his kidneys. "Right," he said, hefting the purse. "So, the usual: GPS locator, telemetry burst transmitter, audio transmitter, power supply."

Harry took the purse and walked off, jerking Gizmo along.

"Harry," Gib called, "If you need to talk—" Harry was gone. "Speak into the purse," said Gib, ruefully and closed the door.

When Omega Sector came into existence, nuclear terrorism was only a possibility. And for years, despite the rise of increasingly well-funded terrorist groups, it remained just that. The construction of a safely transportable nuclear device, simple in theory, required specialized machining equipment, and weapons-grade fissionable materials, both of which were rare and difficult to manufacture or hide. A handful of intelligence organizations were fairly confident they knew the locations of all such machines in the world, and almost all of the weapons-grade heavy metals. Keeping track was a complex, but ultimately attainable goal. So no terrorist groups had risen up brandishing nuclear thunderbolts.

Then the Soviet Union collapsed, and Omega Sector's responsibilities quadrupled almost overnight. So did their funding. But even so, things began to spin out of control. Off-the-rack, ready-made nuclear devices were suddenly available on a burgeoning black market. Four separate ex-Soviet republics had nuclear arsenals, and none of them could afford to keep them, service them, or destroy them. Nuclear-tipped tactical and strategic missiles, thousands of them, became bargaining chips among the republics. They were hoarded, dismantled, shipped across borders, and stolen.

For Trilby and Omega Sector, it was their worst nightmare. And it got worse.

Ten hitherto secret Soviet cities appeared when the curtain came down, all part of a giant industrial complex devoted to nuclear arms production. They had names like Tomsk-7, and Arzamas-16, and until perestroika and glasnost hit them like a runaway train, there were 750,000 technicians and their families inside them, keeping warm and buttering their bread. Not to mention the thousands of military personnel who administered the deployment, security, and actual use of the weapons manufactured.

Like a metastasizing cancer, thousands of hungry atomic mercenaries—scientists and soldiers—were loosed on the world by the fall of the USSR. Thousands of warheads were put into active play on the global chessboard.

As this specter of nuclear chaos rose from the ashes of the Soviet Union, so did the resolve of the superpowers and their allies to keep control. Using both carrots and sticks—political, economic, overt, and covert—they succeeded in their goal for six frantic years.

Until a month ago, when a group of soldiers, led by an ex-Soviet/Kazakh general, hijacked a convoy of ten MIRVs heading back to mother Russia, and came away with four.

And now Salim Abu Aziz was about to lob them into the Great Satan's lap.

But Harry had more important things to worry about. His wife was being pronged by someone other than himself.

There were probably one or two creatures with

shorter life spans, thought Gib. Fruit flies, maybe. He kept his eyes on the van's tracking screen as it slowly scrolled across a map of the city, centering the glowing blip that represented Helen's red Accord.

The blip changed direction at an intersection. "Okay, she's turning on Seventeenth. Make a left, you should see her."

Harry obeyed. "There she is."

Helen pulled into a parking lot beside a Chinese restaurant.

Harry parked, pulled out his giant binoculars, and focused on Helen. She was still in the car, gathering her purse. She pulled down the vanity mirror, touched up her lipstick, then flicked at her bangs a couple of times.

Harry snorted like a disturbed rhino.

Helen got out and walked toward the restaurant, looking around. Harry realized she was checking for a tail. Could she suspect?

"Give me audio," said Harry, putting away the glasses.

Gib switched on his speaker, then potted up the gain. They heard Helen's footsteps, restaurant chatter and clatter.

There was another sound, too, which Gib realized came from inside the van: It was Harry's molars grinding.

Helen walked through the cheesy little dive, all Naugahyde and yellow wallpaper, and approached a booth way in the back.

There sat the dark-haired man Helen knew only as Simon. He was young, and kind of handsome, but what really attracted Helen was the doomed, troubled look in his haggard, unshaven face. Nobody knew the trouble he'd seen.

Simon watched her approach, flicking his eyes behind her, then around the restaurant.

"Are you sure you weren't followed?"

"I kept looking back like you taught me. I didn't see anyone."

He made a conscious effort to relax. "Okay . . . It's just things are a bit hot for me right now. If I get a signal . . ." He held up his cigarette lighter meaningfully. "I may have to leave suddenly."

"I understand."

Simon leaned forward, eyes flickering around the room again. "It's my job to risk my life," he said, sounding apologetic, but quietly and mysteriously desperate. "But not yours. I feel bad about bringing you into this, but you're the only one I can trust."

"Where were you?" she asked, "On a . . . mission?"

"Ssshhh!" said Simon, leaning back. He looked around, reassured himself, then leaned forward again. "We call it an op. Covert operation. And this one got a little rough."

"Worse than Cairo?" she asked, worried and fascinated.

"Cairo was a day at the beach next to this."

"The guy's a spook!" yelled Gib.

"Yeah," said Harry, thunderbolts of death in his eye, "But for who?"

"He could be working her to get you."

Simon's hushed voice came over the speaker. "Did you read the papers yesterday?"

Harry held up his hand for silence.

"Yes," said Helen, nodding at Simon.

"Sometimes a story is a mask for a covert opera-tion. Did you read about the men killed in a mall restroom, and the two men in a running shootout, ending at the Marriott?"

"That was you?"

"You recognize my style. See, you're very good. You're a natural at this."

Gib and Harry stared at each other, jaws dropping.

"This guy's a fake!" screamed Gib.

Helen's voice was breathlessly concerned. "Tell me what happened."

"I'm sorry, I can't," said Simon.

Gib looked up at Harry. "Well, that part's true."

"You can trust me completely," wheedled Helen.

"Yeah, right," commented Harry.

"I know I can," said Simon, contrite, but firm. "But it would compromise your safety too much to know certain things."

"You're right," said Helen, adding, "I was worried when I didn't hear from you."

"It's strange," Simon mused. "I knew I was in a woman's thoughts that night."

"Ha!" said Harry, "more likely in a woman's clothes!"

"Unbelievable," said Gib.

But Helen believed him. "Were they trying to kill you?" she asked.

"Three of them. Hardly worth talking about. Two won't bother me, or the free world, again."

"And you chased one on a horse?"

"Something came over me, I just had to nail him, no matter what the risk. It was pretty hairy. I thought he had me a couple of times. But I really can't take the credit."

"Why not?" asked Helen.

Harry and Gib were on the edge of their seats.

"It's the training," Simon explained. "When a situation like that goes down, I just become a lethal killing machine. I react without thinking."

Gib guffawed. "I'm starting to like this guy!" he said, wiping his eyes.

Harry shot him a dark look.

Gib quickly backpedaled, nodding reassuringly. "Of course, we still have to kill him. That's a given."

Back in the restaurant, Helen leaned even closer across the table, whispering, "What is it you need me to do?"

"Not here. I'll call you and we'll rendezvous again." Simon pulled open the curtains beside him, checking the parking lot. "We have to leave separately, so we aren't seen together. For your safety."

"You'll call me then," pleaded Helen, grabbing her purse.

"Yes. Now go."

Reluctantly she stood, glanced around, and walked off.

Simon leaned out and checked those long legs as they walked away. He made a face like Oww!, then leaned back and let out a pleased and expectant sigh.

Simon, Señor Supercool, cruised down the road in his red vintage Corvette, top down, wind in his hair, accompanying the falsetto chorus of "More Than a Woman" with his own heartfelt castrato stylings.

The street, however, was not lined with adoring

women, but auto repair shops, thrift outlets, and liquor stores.

He pulled into a seedy used-car lot and parked the Vette in its slot right under the fading plastic pennants that lined the street. He reached in the back and pulled out a Day-Glo sign, showing the sale price ($17,995) and stuck it on the dash. Then he hopped out, still singing, and headed for the trailer/office.

Harry pulled the van over half a block away, his eyes lethal black slits. This was too humiliating.

"He's a goddam used car salesman!" Gib laughed. "This just gets better and better. "You gotta admit, Harry, it's funny—"

Harry turned to look at Gib. Apparently he didn't agree.

Gib cleared his throat. "I mean it would be if it was some other idiot instead of you . . . I mean . . . I'm sorry. I know this is painful." Gib heard the molar-grinding sound.

Simon was on the phone to answer one of his pigeons, a boom box on his desk, playing a crude mix of Middle Eastern music and traffic noise.

"It's a great little bar, Amanda. You'd love it. Beirut's a great place if you know the city. Listen, this isn't a secure line. I'll tell you all about it when I get back tomorrow—if I live. . . . Scared? Never. Except of you."

Simon's boss, Doug, seated at the other end of the trailer, noticed something out the window and stood to peer through the blinds.

There was a big guy out there rubbernecking the Vette and glancing at the trailer impatiently.

Doug headed for Simon, fed up.

Simon saw him coming. He lowered his voice, filling it with a life-threatened urgency: "I have to go, baby. A guy's coming toward me—!"

Doug grabbed the phone out of Simon's hand and slammed it in the cradle.

"Simon," said Doug, pointing out the window. "Look out there, into the *real* world. You see that man? Notice how he's looking at the cars. He's called a customer. I know it's been a while, but do you remember what you're supposed to do when we have a customer?"

Simon took a peek. "Oooh, tire-kicker," he said with mock fear. He smoothed his jacket, sprayed Binaca in his mouth, and headed for the door. "Just cut the commission check, Doug. This one's in the fridge."

"It wants you, too," said Simon bouncing jauntily toward Harry. "Feel it vibrate? How about a little spin?"

Harry gave the car a last lingering glance, then nodded soberly. "Okay," he said. He let himself in the passenger side, imagining slamming his door on Simon's fingers, trapping him, then ripping off the creep's leg and beating him to death with it.

Simon leapt over the closed door and started up the Vette. "Rule number one. You gotta jump in." He tossed the price tag into the back. "Ignore that," he said. "We're here to make deals." He dazzled Harry with a devil-may-care smile, and backed out of the slot.

Simon worked hard on his smiles. Each and every night, for a full fifteen minutes, his teeth felt the lash of Pearl Drops. That was followed by ten min-

utes of grin and smile work. Simon's father had
always told him, "A nice smile is money in the bank."

Ironically, it was anger that had killed his father:
He became violently enraged at a Coke machine that
ate his fifty cents. It toppled and crushed him.

Simon swung onto the boulevard and cruised on
down the road, kicking back, grooving to the Vette's
loping thunder.

"See, it's not just the car," he explained, "it's a
total image. An identity you have to go for. This isn't
some high-tech sports car. It doesn't even handle
that great. But that's not the idea, is it." Simon
unleashed his recently perfectly "lascivious sneer."

Harry chuckled dutifully, imagining Simon's head
repeatedly banging off the steering wheel.

Simon continued: "What're we talking about here?
Pussy, right?"

"Absolutely," said Harry.

Simon laughed. Harry laughed. They were
bonding.

"Well, then this is a vital piece of equipment,"
concluded Simon. "Used properly, it can change your
life. See, you cruise. No racing. This ain't a Ferrari.
You check out the scenery, let the scenery check you
out. You got to take it slow. Old cars are like good
women, they heat up fast."

A wink and the *je ne sais quoi* semismile finished
the speech with a cocky flourish.

Harry's mouth smiled back, but his glittering eyes
were actually turned inward, gazing on a scene of
medieval torture.

Simon downshifted two quick gears and pulled
into the parking lot of a taco stand.

* * *

"Let's face it, Harry," said Simon through a mouthful of burrito, "The Vette gets 'em wet. But it's not enough. If you want to really close escrow, you gotta have an angle."

"And you've got one," said Harry, bending over his own Burrito Grande and imagining he was biting off Simon's head.

"It's killer," said Simon. "Look at me—I'm not that much to look at. No, really. I can be honest."

It hadn't actually occurred to Harry to protest.

Simon continued. "But I got 'em lining up. And not just shanks, either."

"So what's your angle?" asked Harry.

"Oh, no." Simon laughed. "Trade secret."

Harry grinned a you dog! sort of grin. "Sure. Set me up and then don't tell me."

"Okay. Just ask yourself: What do women really want? You take those bored housewives, married to the same guy for years. Stuck in a rut. Kids, carpool, grocery shopping, get the car repaired . . . They need some release. Something to break the tedium. The promise of adventure. A hint of danger. I create that for them."

"So you're basically lying your ass off the whole time? I couldn't do it," said Harry, lying his ass off.

"Well, think of it as playing a role," Simon countered. "It's fantasy. You have to work on their dreams. Get them out of their daily suburban grind for a few hours."

"Isn't that hard to keep up in the long run?"

"Doesn't matter. I like change. You know— constant turnover. As soon as I close the deal, it's one or two more times, then adios." Simon favored Harry with one of his most difficult combinations:

the self-reflexive/hellbent quarter-smile with a half-sneer twist.

"Use 'em and lose 'em," said Harry knowingly.

"Exactly," Simon said. "The trick is, you gotta pick your target. They have to be nice little housewife types. Schoolteachers. But, I'm telling you, you get their pilot lit, these babes, they can suck-start a leaf blower."

Harry felt a red pounding in his head. "What about the husbands?" he said with an odd glint in his eye.

"Dickless." Simon snorted contemptuously. If they took care of business, I'd be out of business, know what I mean?"

"Those idiots," said Harry, imagining the front sight of his Glock hooked in one of Simon's nostrils, the hammer slowly going back . . . .

Back on the road, it was Harry in the driver's seat.

"You working on someone right now?" he asked.

Simon smiled like the cat who ate the canary. "Always have a couple on the hook. You know. There's one right now, I've got her panting like a dog. It's great."

Harry's hands tightened on the wheel, and his smile tightened on his face.

"What does she do?"

"You mean at work?" Simon leered.

"Yes," said Harry quietly, pparently missing the joke.

"Paralegal. Married to some boring jerk . . ."

Harry took a corner too fast, making the tires squeal.

". . . And she could be so hot, if she wanted to be. She's like a dying plant that just needs a little water."

Harry, in typical human fashion, bit down on the sore tooth. "But with you, she gets to be hot, right?"

"Red-hot," said Simon, sticking out his tongue and flickering it. "Her thighs steam."

Harry laughed really loud. Then abruptly stopped, took a huge breath, and bit hard on his fist.

Simon saw he was really winding up the big guy's turbofan. Be generous, he thought, make his day. "Yeah, you should see her, she's got the most incredible body. Pair of titties make you want to stand up and beg for buttermilk. Ass like a ten-year-old boy—"

Harry's foot slammed the accelerator to the floor. The Vette leapt forward.

"Whoa!"

"Sooo," began Harry, going for the $64,000 question: "She's pretty good in bed then?"

"Hey, slow down! You're gonna miss the turn!"

Harry spun the wheel right, then left, barreling into the lot at forty miles an hour. He cranked the wheel, hit the emergency brake, and slewed the car into a smoking bootlegger-180. It screeched backward, sliding right into its parking space.

Simon sat bug-eyed for all of two seconds, then blinked with surprised pleasure. "See. You and this car were meant for each other."

He got out, coughed his way through the cloud of tire smoke, and opened Harry's door.

"Why fight it? Sure, I have a couple of other buyers linked up, but I like your style. Whaddaya say? Should we start the paperwork?"

"Let me think about it. Hold it a day for me."

Simon saw doom in those eyes. Heard a bell toll-
ing. He thought it was for the car deal.

"Okay, one day. Because it's you," said Simon, not
quite masking his disappointment.

"Don't worry," said Harry. "You'll see me again."
He walked away.

Weird guy, thought Simon. Looks like he's about
to go postal. Simon headed for the trailer, passing by
Doug who was on his way out.

"I'll be back in twenty minutes. Keep your eye on
the lot, understand?"

"Yes, ma'am!" Simon plodded up the stairs. As
was usual after a failed sale, he was mildly depressed.
He decided to cheer himself up. He picked up the
phone and dialed.

"Helen Tasker, please."

Helen picked up her buzzing phone. "Hello?"

It was Simon, hushed and urgent. "Helen. I need
your help. Can you meet me tonight?"

"What's happened?"

"It's serious. That's all I can say. Just meet me on
R Street, under the Key Bridge. Eight sharp."

The line clicked.

She put the phone down slowly. Simon was in
trouble. She had to help him.

It was 7:45 P.M. and Harry was wrapping it up at his
workstation in Omega Sector.

Gib walked up. "All set?" he asked grimly.

"Yeah," said Harry, standing and slinging on his
coat. "Let me check the taps one more time."

"I just did," said Gib, looking pained and con-
flicted.

"Either your hemmies are bothering you, or you've got bad news."

Gib sighed.

"Give it to me," said Harry.

Gib reached into his pocket and pulled out the transcript. He handed the page to Harry, then took a couple of steps back.

Harry read. His neck corded, his face went red. He dropped the page to the floor, checked his watch, pulled out his Glock, and pumped a round into the breech.

"Easy now, big fella."

"It's almost eight," Harry said calmly.

Six

Harry pulled out of the parking structure onto the gleaming, rain-slicked streets of D.C. He gunned it for the Key Bridge, flipped on the tracking scanner, and selected Helen's transmitter frequency.

The map scrolled rapidly, blurring, settling ten miles away on a quiet street in a Bethesda suburb.

"Waitaminnit. She's still at home!" said Harry with triumph.

"Her purse is, anyway," said Gib.

Harry's face crumpled. Thunderclouds gathered again. He sped even faster, weaving through traffic.

Poor Harry, mused Gib. That obvious possibility would have occurred to him in a microsecond any other time. The big sap was in total denial. It was gumming up his mind.

"Harry, I'm with you every step of the way, understand? But one way or another, we get rid of your little problem tonight. Okay? We have work to do."

Harry looked at his friend. His best friend. He

was putting Gib through hell. Then again, that's
what friends are for.

"Deal," said Harry, bringing the rover up. "Unit
Two? Unit Seven?"

Faisil's voice: "Seven here."

Agent Morton, assigned to Juno's offices, responded: "This is Two."

"Immediate roll," said Harry, startling Gib. "Ac-
quire subject at K Street and Key Bridge. Vehicle is
red-and-white convertible. You have—" he checked
his watch—"six minutes."

"Roger, One. Rolling," said Faisil.

"Copy that," said Morton.

Gib gaped. "Are you out of your mind, Harry? You
can't pull agents off a primary surveillance to follow
your wife! It's gross misappropriation of Sector's resources, it's . . . it's a breach of national security!"

Harry ignored him, intent on cutting off other
drivers. Gib punched Harry in the shoulder.

"Harry! You copy? You've gone too far. You're
losing it big-time." Gib shook his head, definitively.
"I'm sorry, I have to stop you."

"What're you gonna do? Tell on me?"

"Goddammit, Harry, this is our butts! So your life
is in the toilet. So your wife is banging a used-car
salesman. Sure, it's humiliating. But be a man
here—"

"You tell on me, I tell on you."

"Whaddayou mean? I'm clean as a preacher's
sheets, babe. Clean as a—"

"What about that time you trashed a six-week
operation because you were busy getting a blow job?"

Gib's jaw hung open a moment.

"You knew about that?" he said, suddenly contrite.

"Mm-hm," said Harry.

Gib stared out the windshield. "Take Franklin," he said, "it's quicker."

"Attaboy," said Harry, taking the turn, tires squealing.

Gib looked worried. "You don't have any pictures, right? Harry?"

Gib was correct about the purse. Half an hour earlier, while looking in the mirror, Helen had decided her carry-all was shapeless and dowdy. She pulled down a tight, sexy little number from the closet shelf, dusted it off, and strode for the front door.

Dana sat in front of the living room's big-screen TV, channel surfing. In advertising circles, her behavior was more accurately and unflatteringly known as grazing. Truth was, a remote with two alkaline triple-As was just about the level of empowerment she would enjoy as an adult, so what the hell.

Dana looked up as her mother walked by pulling on her nice coat.

"Dinner's in the warmer," Helen said, heading for the door. "Tell your father I may be late."

"Where are you going?" bleated Dana, thrown off balance by this reversal of roles.

"Out," said Helen. And out she went.

She drove down MacArthur Boulevard, the gleaming, moonlit Potomac on her right, and the Key Bridge silhouetted ahead, against the night sky.

She wasn't doing anything wrong, she told herself. She *couldn't* tell Harry about Simon. Simon was a *spy*.

She wondered what kind of trouble Simon was in

this time. She'd helped him out once already, when they'd first met . . . .

She was at the mall, having her usual lunch, a cappuccino and croissant, reading her novel, when she looked up and saw a harried-looking, pale young man watching her intently from a table at the back. He didn't look away. She ducked back into her book, but found she couldn't concentrate. When she glanced up again, he was looking skittishly around the café and mall.

She went back to her book, just a little crestfallen. She'd enjoyed the attention, brief as it was. She would have loved for him to come over, give her some kind of interesting line, ask if he could join her. That's when she'd say, "I'm sorry, I'm married." His eyes would flinch then, with a faraway hurt, a faint but unmistakable echo of some great loss that lay like a wound on his heart. He'd murmur his apologies, in a deep, rumbling voice, bow, and walk away, reluctantly, leaving behind the faint scent of Atkinson's, leather, and tobacco—

Ohmigod. The guy had just sat down *in the seat beside her*.

"Keep this for me," he said, quietly, urgently, sliding a black attaché case against her legs.

He smelled like Irish Spring deodorant soap, and his voice was kind of high, but he was *right there*.

His eyes darted around the mall. "I can't afford to be taken with it. National security is at stake. I'll contact you here Friday, 1300 hours. If I can. If I don't make it, take the briefcase to CIA headquarters in Langley." He turned his spaniel eyes directly on her. "Please help me. Please."

Helen opened her mouth to ask what was going

on, but the young man noticed something behind her, gasped, and took off at a run.

Helen watched him disappear into the crowd. She looked for his pursuers, but couldn't see any *obvious* danger . . . She looked down at the black briefcase, moved her leg around it, and scooted it closer.

She forced herself to be calm. To finish her cappuccino. She scanned the crowd, looking for someone watching her. Then she considered her options carefully. . . . She decided she would do as the stranger asked. Okay. Step two. She had to get back to the office and hide the attaché case. She got up, walked out of the mall, heading back to her office. She had never felt terrified in broad daylight before. It was a new, very odd sensation.

That afternoon, she found her eyes and mind continually wandering to the case stashed under her desk. What if he weren't CIA? There could be anything from a bomb to dirty laundry in there. She had to find out if this guy was on the level.

She pulled out the briefcase, took out a paper clip, and went to work on the locks. Luckily, this was something all law students learned to do their first year. In seconds, the latches were sprung.

Helen opened the case and gasped.

The guy was the real McCoy. A tiny, silver camera was Velcroed to the inside of the upper lid. In the accordion files, she found weathered maps of Beirut and Cairo (the latter with blood on it), and a bound dossier stamped EYES ONLY/TOP SECRET, in which circuit diagrams alternated with pages of pure gibberish: obviously code. In the main compartment, a scuffed holster held a battered Walther P.P.K.

Helen closed the briefcase.

* * *

And three days later, she walked out of her office
with it. She felt so good—so *pumped*—walking
through the mall with it in her hand; then so relieved
and fulfilled seeing the man again, waiting for her
right where they had met.

Simon was deeply grateful, but best of all, he was
proud of her.

"Thank you," he said. "You saved my life. What's
your name?"

"Helen."

"You can call me . . . Simon," he said, his gentle
eyes full of respect. He picked up the attaché case
and checked something on the side, then went completely still.

"You opened it," he said with frightening tone-
lessness.

Helen felt her heart start thumping.

"I just glanced inside."

"This changes everything."

And it had. As Helen turned onto K Street and
headed for the Key Bridge underpass, she felt again
that pleasant mixture of nerves and anticipation that
Simon had come to represent in her lif   t wasn't
love, or even infatuation, and he really wasn't sexy
It was the immediate, visceral excitement of being
part of his life, part of the Big Game. So much of
Helen's own life was about routine and slowly matur-
ing long-term goals—Simon's was a heightened, vola-
tile reality, each second chocked with life-or-death
immediacy. When she was with Simon, she saw
colors and smelled smells she hadn't remembered
were there. She felt like she'd awakened from a
long slumber.

Helen pulled over as she went under the bridge, and stopped near the entrance of a parking lot. She turned off her engine and looked at her watch. A minute after eight. Her hand was shaking. She looked around. The underpass was deserted, scary. No Simon. She waited. He'd said eight sharp. Something must have happened. She reached for her keys. Headlights flashed briefly in the shadows of the lot.

A deep, rumbling engine started up, and then the Vette emerged from the shadows and pulled up beside her.

Simon was inside, motioning for her to get in.

Agent Morton watched the underpass through his light-enhancing nightscope. He saw the woman ditch the Accord and get into the Vette. The Vette drove off, cruising onto a ramp heading up to the bridge.

Morton put his car in gear and followed, picking up his rover. "Two here. Target is southbound on Key Bridge. A man and a woman in the vehicle."

Harry's voice came back. "Roger, Two."

Simon checked his mirrors, staring into them for seconds at a time, pretending he'd spotted a tail.

Helen felt a sick tingle. "Is anything wrong?"

"I'm not sure yet. Now don't be alarmed, but if I'm spotted, it would be best if they don't see you. You should keep your head down until we're out of the city."

He pulled her head down onto his lap, pushing her cheek against his thigh. Simon held her down, loving it.

Gib touched the tracking unit's screen with an electric pencil, flagging points on the scanner's map that represented updated positions for the Vette and the surveilling units.

Morton's voice came out of the rover's speaker: "Jesus. The woman has her head in the guy's lap."

Harry went rigid.

Morton's voice again: "Bone appetit, heh heh."

Gib reached slowly for the rover, careful not to make any sudden moves. "Yo, Two. Just the facts please, over."

"Uh-oh," Simon said, eye on his mirror. "We have a tail."

Helen sat up and peeked over the edge of the seat. The street was empty behind them. Simon pulled her back down.

"No, no! Don't look," he warned.

"I didn't see anything."

"Oh, they're good. They're very good."

"What do we do now?" asked Helen, her spine protesting the unnatural position. Irritation and tedium reared their ugly heads, even in the middle of the Big Game.

"Let's see how good they really are," said Simon. "Hang on!" He cranked the wheel and cut down a side street, tires squealing, fishtailing as he accelerated away.

Faisil, in his surveillance van, saw the Vette charge past; going the opposite way. He scooped up his handset.

"Seven here. Target now eastbound on Wilson. I think he's getting hinky."

Gib checked the map. "Okay, Seven, hand it off. We'll pick them up when they reach Grand." Up ahead, the Vette flashed by, charging through an intersection.

It was like the red cape to a bull. Harry gunned it, nostrils dilated, eyes bugging, veins standing out like lightning in a thunderstorm.

Gib keyed the rover again. "We have the ball," he said, then held on as Harry took the turn and slid in line a safe distance behind the Vette.

Simon was milking it for every drop. He cut down another road, checked his mirror.

"Oh, you're sly," he said. "You're so sly."

Helen peered behind her, unable to see—

"You better keep your head down," said Simon, pushing her into his lap again. "They might open fire." He cut the wheel sharply and barreled down an alley.

"Shit!" said Harry. The guy really was driving as though he'd made the tail.

"Go around," said Gib, "Take the next right!"

But Simon doubled back, and a few moments later the Vette thundered onto an expressway heading toward the outskirts of Arlington. Simon had actually lost them.

He let Helen up, glancing in his rearview with an acid smile composed of equal parts disgust and contempt.

"So predictable," he sniffed. "I'm almost disappointed."

Helen groaned and leaned back as her spine relaxed.

Simon thought it was terror that had exhausted her.

"Don't worry," he said, sliding his face into a gentle, fatherly crinkle, an interesting smile because it's done mostly with the eyes. "They're clumsy tonight."

And that is indeed how Omega Sector's finest felt. Except for Harry, who had moved beyond apoplectic into apocalyptic.

"Two! Do you have eyeball?" he roared.

"Negative. No visual."

"Seven! Report!"

"Seven here. Don't have them, over."

Harry keyed his rover one more time. "One to Condor. Are you on station yet? Condor? Do you copy?"

A highway drifted lazily over the grassy hills at the edge of Arlington County. The Vette crested a hill and coasted down through the sparsely populated grazing land. A moment later, a helicopter rose from behind the hill, moonlight gleaming off its back fuselage. It pitched forward, rotors strangely muted in a low-power whisper mode.

Harry relaxed as he heard the pilot's voice: "This is Condor. We have the ball, repeat, we have a good lock-up on I.R."

The tiny pair of red eyes reflecting the Vette's headlights were too small to be a cat's. They winked out as the creature scurried deeper into the shadows under the decrepit, single-wide mobile home that Simon had just parked in front of.

Helen shuddered, wondering who lived there. Maybe it was some seedy, low-life drunk who manufactured false identity papers during his brief bouts of sobriety. Maybe it was a toothless paranoic who cursed the Pope while he sold untraceable black market weaponry. She turned to Simon, her face an eloquent question mark.

"My house in the city is too hot right now. So is the penthouse in New York. But this place is secure."

It was smelly, too. Was that mildew? wondered Helen, trying not to let Simon hear her sniff. Actually, it was a medley of molds (some of them quite rare), vermin spoor, and unwashed laundry.

Simon wished he could spritz the room with his hair spray, but he comforted himself with the fact that in a minute or two Helen's nose would stop sending the redundant warning signals to her brain and she would forget. He just had to brazen it out for a minute. Create distractions.

Simon clicked on some cool jazz, already cued. The music slid tinnily out of a square, beige speaker, last seen on a high school classroom's wall.

As Helen ran her eyes over the stained bedspread, Simon unscrewed the cap on a bottle of red he'd cellared the day before and poured for them both.

Helen forced herself not to peer closely at the glass he handed her. If she had, she would have seen a picture of a galloping horse and the name of the local racetrack that had given the glass away as a promotion.

"To our assignment," he said and clinked glasses.

"What is it you need me to do?" she asked, pretending to sip.

"I want you to be my wife," he said, pretending not to realize how dramatic that sounded.

"I'm married!" Helen said.

"Just for the operation in Paris. I need to be married. They'll be looking for a man traveling alone."

"We're going to Paris?" She decided she needed a drink, no matter what was in her glass.

"Helen, there's a double agent in my outfit. I don't know who. There's no one I can trust. Except you. Can you get away? Just for two days?"

"I don't know. I have to think about it."

"Here. Sit down. Be comfortable," said Simon, clearing a place for her on the bed. She sat. Simon topped off her glass.

Harry, Gib, and three other Sector agents, all dressed in black jumpsuits, slung on battle harnesses in perfect unison, then slipped black ski masks over their heads. Harry swung up his MP-5 and led them out from behind a billboard, marching in quick time.

"One to Condor," said Harry into his subvocal transceiver. "Give us some light."

The suppressed *thwoop-thwoop* of the helicopter faded in as it descended into position and splashed a brilliant oval of blue light onto the dirt in front of Harry's team.

Harry and his team closed on the trailer. For the first time in days, Harry looked happy.

Helen was thinking hard. But in the end, all she had to do was imagine how she'd feel a month from now if she said no.

She looked at Simon and nodded slowly. "Okay. I'll do it."

Simon took her hand in his and looked into her eyes. "You just saved my life. You are so incredibly brave," he said with the same pride he'd showed the day she brought him the attaché case. "I have to remind myself the fear you must be feeling. I've lived like this for years, so I'm used to it. Fear is not an option, for me. Every day when I get up, I think it might be my last. But it makes you appreciate life. And the *moment*. Because that may be all you have."

Simon paused to emphasize that point. Something about it was important to him, she realized. Simon leaned closer.

"Helen, to pull this cover story off, we have to look exactly like two people who are intimate with each other. The enemy can spot a fake easily."

Simon dropped a hand on her knee. Helen tensed up immediately.

"You see what I mean?" said Simon. To give him his due, he was a canny swine. "That reaction would give us away in a second." He ladled out a soothing, reassuring smile, again doing most of the work with his eyes. Thousands of cheek-raises had paid off with premature crow's-feet, and he used them now, sensing it was time to pull out all the stops.

"Try to relax," he said.

Helen nodded nervously. "It's just that . . . it's been sixteen years since anyone but Harry did that, I—"

"Breathe, breathe. That's better. Let yourself slip into the role."

Simon put his arm around her shoulder and pulled her toward him. Helen couldn't believe it. She

strained backward as he pulled her slowly down onto
the bed.

"There you go," he said. "That's right."

He pulled against her, putting his lips on hers.
She made a little protest sound, and pushed against
him. But not hard enough.

He slid his hand up her thigh. His fingers, stroking
in little circles, slipping under her skirt—

"No! Stop!" yelled Helen, pushing hard against
his chest.

But Simon kept pulling at her, extending his
puckered lips as far as they would go.

"Get off me right now!" Helen screamed, getting a
knee between his legs and bringing it up sharply.

"Oof!" grunted Simon, getting quickly off her.
Helen pulled her knees up and got her elbows under
her, staring daggers at him.

"What is wrong with you?"

He pleaded with his puppy dog eyes. "If not for
me, then for democracy," he whined.

Kabloooey!

Tiny shaped charges blew off the entire end wall
of the trailer, opening it like a can of Spam—and
incidentally knocking Simon forward, right between
Helen's legs. They both yelled and stared toward the
new opening in the trailer.

Backlit by a chopper's xenon, five evil-looking
commandos led by a muscular giant swarmed inside,
swinging machine-pistols and flashlights.

The leader's flashlight found the bed, illuminating
the stunned couple: Helen's knees were up on either
side of Simon's hips. Helen screamed bloody murder,
which is exactly what Harry had in mind.

But Simon couldn't say a word. After all those

years of bullshitting, here it was. Genuine commandos had caught him trying to bang another man's
wife, and they were ripping his place to shreds. He
blinked in the beam of the copter's searchlight,
smoke and dust from the rotor-wash choking him, a
giant man coming toward him, and he realized he
was going to die. And he knew it was for lying. His
mother had always told him, "If you lie, devils will
drag you down to Hell and torture you for eight
million years."

Ironically, it was a lie that had killed his mother.
A mugger had accosted her at a bus stop and said,
"Give me your money." Without even taking the
cigarette out of her mouth, she had replied, "I don't
have any money, asshole." The mugger had pushed
her in front of a serendipitously arriving bus.

And now her orphan, Simon, felt an iron claw grip
his neck. The giant dude lifted him with one arm,
and dragged him backward out of the trailer, choking
off any protests Simon might have made.

Gib meanwhile was dragging Helen outside. She
bit, hit, slapped, kicked—Gib couldn't believe it. He
almost yelled her name. He grabbed her wrists, but
she kneed him in the calzones, leapt out of the
trailer, and ran shrieking into the trees.

Harry tossed Simon into the arms of one of his
men and lit out after her, followed by his backup,
Agent Keough. He caught Helen in the trees and put
her in a headlock.

"Ow! You—" Helen sunk her teeth deep into
Harry's arm.

"Owwww!" he screamed letting go.

Helen ran for it. Agent Keough, responding exactly as he was trained to, ran her down and clipped her on the head with the butt of his weapon.

He didn't understand why Harry punched his lights out.

Agent Keough led Helen, hooded and handcuffed, into the interrogation room in Omega Sector: an empty rectangle with a single stool set under a caged light. Keough sat her down, unlocked her cuffs, and ran.

Helen whipped off her hood and blinked, dazzled by the harsh light. She heard the door click shut and ran to it, pulling on the handle.

"Let me out!" She banged her fist on the door. It hurt, and brought no response. She noticed one wall of the room was a mirror. She crossed to it, trying to peer through to the other side.

"Is there someone in there?"

"Sit down!" boomed a big, harsh, weirdly inhuman voice.

In a dark room on the other side, Harry and Gib sat in front of microphones connected to digital distortion circuitry. Speakers brought them Helen's defiant voice:

"Who are you?!"

Harry keyed his mike again. "I said *sit down!*"

Helen glowered, but this time she obeyed. She figured she'd get the show on the road.

"Who do you work for?" said the big voice.

"Kettleman, Barnes and McGrath," Helen said. "I'm a paralegal."

"Of course you are, Mrs. Tasker," said the voice. "And what were you doing with the international terrorist, Carlos the Jackal?"

"Checking his briefs?" said a second, more rapid voice.

She heard a quick thud before the mike was turned off. What was going on in there?

"He told me he was an American agent," she said.

"How long have you been a member of his faction?" said the first voice.

"I don't know anything about a faction. I just met Simon—or whatever his name is—a couple of weeks ago. I barely know him."

The fast-talking voice said, "That's not what it looked like when we found you."

Helen flushed, remembering.

"How did you meet him?" bellowed the big voice.

Helen told them the story of the attaché case. Harry and Gib shook their heads in disbelief. This Simon guy was primordial sleaze.

"Why did you continue to see him?" asked Harry.

"He needed my help," she answered.

"Not because you were attracted to him?"

"No."

"You weren't attracted to him at all?" pressed Harry.

"Well . . . He's sort of cute."

Harry went purple.

"Count to ten," said Gib, and keyed his mike: "Is this a common thing for you? Cheating?"

"No! Never!"

"So it was your first time," wheedled Gib.

"I wasn't cheating!"

Harry was breathing again. He keyed his mike.

"Tell me about your husband, Mrs. Tasker."

"He's a . . . He owns the Microsoft Corporation.

And he's going to have you killed when I tell him about this."

The big voice came on, flat and menacing: "He's a sales rep for a computer company, Mrs. Tasker. And if you ever want to see him or your daughter again, you will answer the rest of our questions with total honesty."

Helen froze. Dana. Harry. Bastards! Utter bastards—

"Now tell the truth," said the big voice, "Would you say your husband was boring?"

What? Jesus . . . Honestly . . . "Yeah. I suppose he is," she said.

The fast talker spoke up: "So sex with him isn't exactly making your flag wave anymore."

That strange thudding sound again. This was too weird. "That's none of your goddam business!" yelled Helen. "What kind of questions are these?"

The big voice boomed, trying to intimidate her. "You're in a lot of trouble, Mrs. Tasker! I suggest you cooperate, even if we want to know the most intimate details of your life."

Helen glowered at the mirror. Chicken shits! She was becoming more and more enraged at their threats, and truth be told, hurt and raw at what they were pulling out of her. She fought back, against them, and herself.

"My husband is a good man." The woman she saw reflected in the mirror was full of anguish.

The fast talker: "But he's not exactly ringing your bell lately, right? I mean—"

On the other side of the mirror, Harry covered Gib's mike with a giant hand. *"Do you mind?"*

Gib put up both hands. "Just trying to get to the

bottom of things, Harry." Gib sat back, pleased that
he'd been able to pay Harry back for two days of hell.

Harry let his eye linger on Gib a moment as he
keyed his own mike. "Why did you go to Carlos's
hideout, Mrs. Tasker?"

"He wanted me to go with him on a mission, to
pose as his wife."

"And you agreed?"

"Yes," she said, looking down.

Harry gaped at her. Who was this woman on the
other side of the mirror? He truly was Through The
Looking Glass, he thought. He was completely disori-
ented.

"Why?" he finally asked.

"I don't know. I guess I needed something
that . . ." Her voice trailed away.

"What? What did you need?"

She took a good look in the mirror. And forgave
herself.

"I needed to feel alive. I wanted to do something . . . *outrageous*." She kept looking and saw it
went even deeper than that: "It felt good to be
needed. To be trusted. To be special." Helen found
that her throat was hurting her, and her eyes were
swelling and feeling hot. "The sand's running out of
the hourglass, you know. I wanted to be able to look
back and say: See. I did that! It was wild and it was
reckless and outrageous—and I *fucking did it*!"

Harry stared at his wife. No, not "his wife." At a
person named Helen. He let out a deep sigh, utterly
deflated. No argument here, he thought.

But there was one last issue to be settled. One
that was very important to Harry. And crucial to the
continued health of Simon the Sleazebag.

"This Simon. Did you sleep with him?"

"No," said Helen flatly.

Gib was suspicious: "Maybe they were awake the whole time, know what I mean?"

Harry looked at his friend like he was a roach—and then he reached out and keyed the mike.

"Let me rephrase that. Did you have sexual relations with him?"

"Look, you jerk, if you're going to ask me everything four times, this is going to take forever. I have to get home to my family."

"Answer the question!" demanded the booming voice.

Helen stood up, trembling with rage, clenching her fists. "Let me out of here!" she screamed. "Let me out of here right now you chicken-shit bastards!" She grabbed her stool and charged toward the mirror, swinging with all her might. *Wham!*

"I didn't sleep with him!" she shrieked. *Wham!* "You hear me you—" *Blam!*

"Please stop, Mrs. Tasker," said the calm, fast-talking voice. "It's unbreakable."

Crack! The mirror starred from side to side with huge cracks.

Gib jumped up, moving away from the glass, and the out-of-control woman only inches from his face.

"Maybe she's telling the truth," he allowed, feeling suddenly generous.

"Wait! Calm down, Mrs. Tasker. There is only one more question."

Helen, exhausted by now, dropped the stool and stood there panting.

"What?" she yelled bitterly.

"Do you still love your husband?"

Helen broke down. "Yes," she said through her sobs.

"I didn't hear you."

"Yes! I love him. I've always loved him. And I always will love him—" The sobbing took over for a moment, then she controlled herself and wiped her eyes. "Can I go home now, please?" Assholes.

Harry's eyes were red, too.

Gib looked at him. "She loves ya. Now what."

Harry was thinking. Helen wanted excitement, intrigue, a secret life all her own. He'd provide it for her. He keyed his mike.

"There is only one solution to your problem, Mrs. Tasker. You must work for us."

Gib looked at Harry. Uh-oh, blown head gasket. "Harry, what're you doing?"

"I'm giving her an assignment," he explained, as if to an idiot. To Helen, he said: "You will work for us just once. And then you must retire, forever. The choice is simple. If you agree, we will drop the charges against you, and you can go back to your normal life. If you refuse, you will go to federal prison and your husband and daughter will be left humiliated and alone. Your life will be destroyed. Well?"

"Oh, gee, let me see, hmmm . . ." Helen wished she had a bazooka.

"Yes or no, Mrs. Tasker."

"Of course I'm going to do it, you bozo. What's involved?"

Gib winced. Harry had taken more of a beating tonight than on any mission they'd ever been on. That must be it, thought Gib. He's suffered permanent mental damage. Textbook case of falling out of your tree.

Harry spoke into his mike. "You will be contacted with the assignment."

"My husband can't know about this," she warned.

"No one must know!" boomed the voice. "Especially him. You must appear to live your life normally, conveying nothing. The security of this nation depends on it."

She'd heard that one before.

"Can you do that?" said the voice.

"I think so."

"Think carefully. You will be lying to the man you love. The person who trusts you the most."

"I can do it," said Helen without hesitation. After what she'd been through that night, lying to her husband seemed like a relaxing vacation.

"The code name of your contact will be Boris," the voice informed her. "Your name will be—"

"Natasha?" prompted Helen hopefully.

"No," said Harry, "Doris."

Helen tossed a disbelieving look through the shattered glass, hoping Bozo would catch it. Doris. Puhleeze. What a loser.

Inside, Harry threw up his hands and stood to go. "Now she doesn't like her code name. She's gonna start smashing the window again." He headed for the door.

"Wait for me," said Gib, hurrying after him. In all seriousness, both of them had developed a deep and surprised respect for Helen's destructive powers.

Unit Seven rolled into the shadows under the Key Bridge and stopped next to Helen's Accord. The side door slid back and hands gently steadied the hooded Helen as she stepped onto the asphalt beside the van. The black-gloved hands handed her her purse, turned her so that she faced away, then whisked off her hood.

Helen spun around in time to see the door slide shut as the van sped away.

She looked around. Nothing. No one. Under a dark bridge. In the middle of the night. A few hours ago this same situation had made her skin crawl.

"Yes!" she yelled, pumping her fist. She hurried to her car.

Harry and Gib's van drove into the Blue Ridge, and turned onto a recently resurfaced side road that wound up into the Massanutten Mountains. The van stopped at a gate in a high, sturdy run of cyclone fencing topped by a helix of razor wire.

Harry, still in his commando rig, jumped out of the van and picked the lock on the gate, apparently not seeing the red-lettered sign that said, DANGER. KEEP OUT. NO TRESPASSING. VIOLATORS WILL BE PROSECUTED. A faint rumbling roar filled the air, more felt than heard. *Click.* Harry pushed the gate open and jumped back in the van.

Gib drove up the winding access road to an overlook parking lot. The side door opened and a pair of big gloved hands pushed the hooded Simon out of the van. Simon heard it immediately, a deep, thundering rumble, very loud. What the hell was that?

Harry and Gib, now wearing ski masks, marched Simon across the asphalt parking lot. Then he felt rocky dirt under his feet. The thundering sound was overwhelming now. Simon could feel a cool, moist wind on his hands. The men stopped pushing. His hood slid off. His heart flopped on its side. And he screamed.

"Aaaaaaaaaaaagh!"

Merciless hands held him rock steady over the very edge of a monumental abyss fronting an hydroelectric dam. Six hundred feet below, bone-crushing torrents of water roiled into a plunge pool, then calmed themselves in a stilling basin and drifted away down a narrow rocky gorge.

"You son of a bitch," Harry growled. "Did you really think you could elude us forever, Carlos?"

"Wait!" Simon croaked. "You got the wrong guy! My name's Simon!" He twisted around, desperate to look at them. If they saw his face, were confronted with his humanity (such as it was) maybe they would spare him—

"Look, just let me go! There's no need to kill me, I haven't seen your—"

Harry whipped off his ski mask.

"—face!" bleated Simon, almost fainting. "Shit! Shit!" he mewled, ducking his head as Harry pulled his hair, forcing him to look. Then Simon recognized him.

"Hey! It's you!" In the presence of a customer, the ancient instinct to sell overpowered him. "You still interested in that Vette at all?"

Gib took off his mask and stepped forward. "You can drop it now, Carlos. The game is over. Your career as an international terrorist is too well documented."

Harry pushed till Simon's feet dangled over the edge.

"No! I sell cars! That's all! Not even foreign cars. Nothing international, I swear. I'm no terrorist.

Everything I said was a lie! You have to believe me!
I'm actually a complete coward. If anyone ever pulled
a gun on me I'd—"

Harry whipped his Glock out and snapped the
muzzle down right in front of Simon's eyes.

"—faaaaiint! Don't kill me! I'm not a spy! I'm
nothing. I'm navel lint." Simon began to hyperventi-
late and whimper. "I have to *lie* to women to get laid.
And I don't score much. Really . . ."

Two pairs of sneering, implacable eyes stared down
at him.

Simon began to blubber in fear. "And I have a
really small penis. It's pathetic . . . Oh, God . . ."
Simon glanced down at his pants, laughing and
sobbing at the same time. "Look! See? Would a spy
pee himself?"

Harry had had enough. He yanked Simon away
from the edge. "Beat it," he said and gestured with
his gun.

Simon froze, then his face crumpled again. "Oh,
no. Soon as I turn around you'll shoot me!"

Harry and Gib shared a disgusted look. They
started for the van. Simon followed like a dog.

"You're gonna shoot me, I know it! Please don't.
You can have the car for free!"

Gib spun around and pumped three rounds into
the ground at Simon's feet, forcing him to dance
backward.

"Aaagh!"

"Take off, dipshit," said Gib.

They got into the van and drove away, leaving
Simon behind. Simon raised his face to the heavens,
weeping thankfully.

"Mom, I swear I'll never lie again," he said, telling
the first lie of the rest of his life.

Seven

After the Harry-Aziz Wild West Show at the Marriott, Juno Skinner dropped out of sight. Her gallery still operated, but the proprietress was nowhere to be found. And nothing out of the ordinary went in or out of her offices or showroom as far as Omega Sector could tell, and their surveillance was complete. Even a couple of covert break-ins had turned up nothing except two legally registered semi-automatic handguns used by Juno's private security guards.

The trail on Aziz had also gone cold. Faisil traced the rental station wagon that Aziz and his two thugs had used. It had been rented to a Mr. Ali Abu Muhammad, whose passport identified him as a citizen of the rather unthreatening United Arab Emirates. No such person showed up on INS or U.S. Customs computers.

Faisil ran Aziz's name, and all of his known associates, through every intelligence and law-enforcement network at his disposal: INS, Customs, CIA, NSA, FBI, the Pentagon/Armed Forces networks, DEA, and the Coast Guard. Six of the names showed up as having been in the United States in recent years, but none was in the United States at present.

Faisil set up a priority alert at ten other cooperative corporate and private intelligence networks, flagging Aziz, his associates, Juno Skinner, and Crimson Jihad. Sector liaison agents scattered east and west to brief the Japanese, Mossad, MI-6, the Sureté, and several other friendly intelligence agencies in Europe and the Mideast. All of them began round-the-clock efforts to scrape up information on Aziz and the Crimson Jihad.

While Faisil searched and downloaded, Gib and Harry collated and organized what turned out to be an ominous profile. Most of the warlords and strongmen of the Mideast struggled for local power and influence. But the Crimson Jihad had more grand, more global, Pan-Arabic ambitions. Aziz was not a demagogue manipulating the unstable passions of a nationalistic rabble. He didn't work for the approval of a crowd of cannon fodder. He worked in the service of an abstraction. He saw himself as no less than the Sword of Islam.

The West, and now America, had trampled on Islam for long enough. The United States's New World Order—American dominance of the Mideast and Third World—must be destroyed. The means, the power to reshape the world more equitably was there. It needed only someone with the boldness to grasp that power and the will to wield it.

It sounded megalomaniacal. But what made Aziz

so formidable was his mixture of militant political extremism and utterly pragmatic opportunism. With the rank and file, he flew the flag of a bloodthirsty religious fanatic. But with the wealthy and powerful people who financed and supported his efforts, he talked dollars and cents, analyzed historical, economic, and ideological forces, and forecasted geopolitical events. And they trusted him. He had trained himself well.

Aziz was born the scion of a wealthy Syrian family living in Beirut. By the age of sixteen, he spoke five languages, including Japanese. But his true love and nearly constant companion was history and those philosophies that sought to understand the worldline of human culture. Hesiod, Locke, Hegel, Nietszche, Marx, Foucault—Aziz devoured them all. One Swiss boarding school teacher described him as "simply the most brilliant and dedicated student I ever had."

In 1977, almost overnight, a confluence of inner and outer events changed his life forever. He had started at Oxford, intending to embark on a career as an academic. Almost immediately he became restless and bored with his chosen vocation. His passionate, original, Arab-centered theorizations circulated in dimly lit caverns, read by dusty, impotent dons and myopic hair-splitters who knew only books, not *history*.

Outside in the real world, it was the end of an earth-shaking decade in Middle-Eastern/global history: the rise of the Oil Cartel, and the beginnings of a militantly resurgent Islam.

And then, his parents were murdered. The Marines who killed them blamed it on "incontinent ordnance" sprayed from a Cherokee assault copter during a firefight with Christian Phalangists. A mistake, they said. His parents had been in the wrong place at the wrong time.

It all came together. Aziz, overnight, dedicated himself to proving that it was not his parents, but the United States who had been in the wrong place at the wrong time.

Orphaned and angry, Aziz joined the faction of a Lebanese Marxist guerrilla in Beirut, a man who believed that the Muslim community must war against all adversaries equally, Christian, American, or Jewish.

Aziz's first taste of blood came when he strapped dynamite inside a tire and rolled it down a hill into a group of inattentive Phalangists.

He rose to second in command, then split with his leader, who advocated suicide missions that took innocent lives. To Aziz, publicity seemed a contemptible, unworthy goal for a warrior. In retaliation for the split that took some of his fiercest fighters, the Marxist leader kidnapped two of Aziz's closest comrades, tortured them, killed them, and sent a videotape of it all to Aziz.

Aziz, who had gone underground in France by then, saw that he was a rank amateur when it came to the Middle East's hardball tribal politics. He put out feelers, and started talking with the PLO, searching for the political means to advance his faction's cause. He got the giant's attention, and a hint of favor. He was immediately set up and betrayed by an Arafat rival. Framed for a conspiracy to blow up a Turkish diplomat, he spent the next four years in a brutal, racist French prison.

But Aziz was never one for sorrow. He tempered

his will in a black pool of rage. He studied—military history and theorists of power. And he wrote letters, reams and reams of them. He walked out of prison in 1988, hearing a rumbling from the Berlin Wall. He had predicted it would fall.

And it did. It meant more to Aziz than just a vindication of his historical analyses. It made him realize that only a single, great, dramatic event, one as momentous as the crumbling of the Iron Curtain, would make the world sit up and take fearful, respectful notice of a powerful, resurgent Islam. Such an act would require a great and single-minded will, like the one Aziz had painfully forged in that French hellhole.

Aziz came out of prison with one other very important thing. His pen pals. A broad array of international contacts who knew and understood the greatness of his mind, and of his goals. They guided him to the powerful and moneyed individuals who shared his geopolitical objectives.

With the benefit of very deep individual pockets, and a couple of national treasuries to support him, Aziz handpicked an ultrahardline group of berserkers, who fearlessly embarked on their suicide training knowing that, though there might be no Paradise waiting for them, their names would live on, uttered by generations of Arab children whenever and wherever the story of the New Islamic World was told. They were ready—the dumber ones even *eager*—to martyr themselves. This was truly *jihad*, a Holy War of Blood. Arafat, Abu Nidal, Hussein, Qaddafi—they were stooges, cowards, greedy.

Crimson Jihad was the one truly righteous instrument of Islam's will to power.

* * *

And while Harry and Gib studied and learned, and Omega Sector's search continued without success, a nascent holocaust crossed into United States territorial waters: four swaddled nightmares, wedged deep in the hold of a small, heavily laden freighter, steaming toward the Florida Keys.

So close. Aziz forced himself to remain calm. He updated his list of every possible threat, mistake, and misfortune that could possibly befall his operation. He methodically addressed each one. He was a perfectionist, hated loose ends, clutter, lack of control. And there was one loose end that particularly bothered him. "Renquist."

Harry looked up from the tracking screen and over at Gib. "Relax. It's lunch hour, right? We've got nothing to do anyway."

Gib shook his head, picking his way through the light, suburban traffic. "We made a deal, Harry."

"That was for Helen. This is for Dana."

Gib sighed. They were his family, too. "If we're the last line of defense, this country's in trouble."

Harry watched the blip on the screen. "We should pick up visual at the next light."

The scrambler phone in Harry's briefcase rang. Harry opened it.

ID POS/TRILBY, SPENCER. Oh shit.

"Morning, boss."

Trilby had his mouth right up to his speaker, giving his voice a sepulchral intimacy. "Harry, this report on last night's operation is the most transparent fabrication I've ever seen even, even from you. I'm sure you won't mind giving me a little more detail on why all these assets were deployed."

"Last night? Absolutely, sir. But can it wait? I'm on a critical surveillance right now."

Just ahead, Trent and Dana zipped through the intersection, weaving through cars.

Harry snapped his fingers and waved for Gib to hurry, then whipped out his monstrous, gyro-stabilized binoculars. Gib took the turn and pulled in behind the Yamaha.

"Harry, is there anything you want to tell me?" Trilby asked.

"No, sir. Not that I can think of." Harry noticed the little Trent fuck wore his retro Converse without socks. Phew!

"Harry?"

"Yes, sir," he answered, distracted.

"You know we never fire anybody."

Harry slowly let the binoculars fall, the phone still pressed to his ear. Click.

Harry put back the phone, slowly.

"We're dead," said Gib.

"Yeah," said Harry. But first things first.

Harry walked by a warehouse's roll-up door, passing Trent's Yamaha parked with some other motorcycles and scooters, and a few beat-up, primer-splashed American classics that all needed oil changes and air in the tires.

Whatever happened to motorheads? wondered Harry like a grumpy old fart. Or going to school on a Wednesday. They're all "putting together a look" and starting garage bands, he snorted.

Which is exactly what Dana, Trent, and her friends had done.

The cavernous warehouse lent a natural reverb to

their punchy cover of Cream's "Sunshine Of Your Love." And it was Dana belting out the lyrics. She worked the mike and the stage with a natural grace, and she was gifted with the most important singing talent of all: truthfulness. You believed her when she sang.

Harry slid behind a pillar and peeked toward the stage, staring curiously at his daughter. He hadn't seen Dana look this full of life since she was a tiny child.

As with Helen the night before, he could barely recognize her.

He remembered his lesson, the one he'd learned from interrogating Helen. This was not "his daughter." This was a person named Dana with her own powerful desires, and a life, both inner and outer, independent of Harry or her place in their family.

Then again, she *was* his daughter. And she was going to get an education.

Harry's hand reached out and pulled the master circuit breaker. *Thunk.* The warehouse plunged into darkness and the music cut off. The drums petered out, and then Trent's tinny, unamplified guitar strumming quit, too. The audience of partying kids groaned.

The metal door of the warehouse rolled up, blinding the kids with sunlight. A big, shadowy figure, backlit by the glare, marched forward toward the stage.

It pointed at Dana. "You," said the voice. "Come with me."

"Oh, my Gooood!" It was her dad, and he was about to drag her away in front of all her friends!

Harry marched his daughter across the parking

lot, found a comfortable-looking pile of industrial junk and sat her angry, sulky ass down. She wouldn't look at him, but Harry didn't care. Just be straight with her, he thought. That's all you need to do.

"There are going to be some changes, Dana. You're going to start following some rules. And I'm going to be there to see that you do."

"Yeah, right."

Her venom made him sad, but it was also encouraging. It told him that his neglect had hurt her: Maybe his future attentions would have an equally strong, but positive effect.

Harry continued: "You're going to stay in school. Do you understand?"

"Why? So I can end up like you? What's the point?"

Harry looked at her with deep and gentle empathy. Dana did a double take. She was expecting lightning and thunder, but instead she got first snow.

Harry pushed the hair back from her face.

"Did I tell you about the time we first met? You were quite young at the time. All wet and still attached to your mom by a cord. You opened your eyes and looked right at me. And I knew then I would always love you with all my heart."

Dana looked up at her dad, at his gently smiling face so obviously full of love for her. A black cyclone of loneliness and confusion melted away inside her, leaving behind a single hurt cry. She threw her arms around her father's waist and hugged him, fiercely.

He stroked her hair, his own eyes brimming with tears. "Somewhere along the way," said Harry, "I got lost. I forgot about what was really important. I'm sorry, pump—I mean—"

Dana hugged him even tighter. She felt his strong arms go around her and press her against his chest. They stayed holding each other for a while. Then when Harry felt Dana's arms relax a little, he said, "Dana, about your singing . . ."

Dana pulled back slowly and wiped her eyes. She knew what was coming.

Harry smiled. "You were pretty good!"

"You think so?"

"Yeah," he said, grinning.

Gib, Harry, and Dana sang raucously and loudly as they drove Dana back toward her school. "I've been waiting so long / To be where I'm going / In the sunshine of your lo-o-o-o-ove!"

They nailed the sustain like pros, whooped it up and slapped high fives.

"How come you guys know the words?" asked Dana.

"That song came out in 1968, when I was exactly your age," explained Harry.

Dana gaped, then her lip curled in a sneer. "Unbelievable! Trent told me he wrote it."

Gib snorted, pulling over to the curb in front of the school.

"He's history," Dana muttered. She kissed her dad, grabbed her book bag and walked away, heading for class.

The Taskers were getting better at family dinners. Harry and Dana, especially, were feeling frisky, teasing each other and showing off healthy appetites. Helen laughed at them, pleasantly surprised, but she herself was still half in shadow, waiting for word from Bozo or Boris or whoever it would be.

"I'm done." said Dana, having eaten half of the food on her plate. A record. She stood up, then turned and—*remembered her manners*.

"May I be excused?" she asked.

Harry choked on some chicken gristle.

Helen gaped at Dana, waiting for the giant burp that would signal it was all a joke. Dana just stood there, waiting.

"Y-yes, of course," quavered Helen. Something was suspicious here. "Where are you off to, young lady?"

"Nowhere. I have a book report," she said, pointing to her room. Dana walked away.

Helen looked at Harry. He gave an exaggerated shrug.

They went back to their dinners.

"So last night was pretty exciting, huh?"

Helen, caught off guard, blanched in fear. "What?"

"The flat tire."

"Oh! The flat tire! Yeah, I thought the damn tow truck was never going to get there."

"You should have called me. I don't mind."

The phone rang. Harry, cruelly, started to get up.

"I'll get it!" chirped Helen, hurrying to cut him off.

She hurried into the kitchen and picked up the receiver.

"Hello?"

A processed, metallic voice. "Doris?" A strange crunching sound, like static followed his speech.

"Hi, Allison," said Helen cheerily, glancing toward the kitchen doorway.

"What?" said the robotic voice.

God, these people were morons. "Go *ahead*, I'm listening."

More rhythmic static. "Listen carefully . . ."

Duh! The guy was probably standing inside a Cone of Silence, talking into his shoe.

"You are to go to the Hotel Marquis in one hour. Pick up an envelope marked "Doris" at the front desk. And dress sexy."

"What?"

"Get going!"

Back at Omega Sector, Gib hung up his phone, smiled, and popped another potato chip in his mouth.

Helen, meanwhile, stared at the phone, desperately adlibbing: "Uhm, well, okay then. You sound terrible. I'll run out right now. Just call the prescription in to the pharmacy. Sure. No problem. 'Bye."

Helen walked into the dining room and picked up her plate. Harry shoved a piece of bread in his mouth, hiding a smile.

"Allison is sick in bed. I have to go over there, honey."

"Sure, hon." Harry stood. "Let me drive you."

"No! . . . I mean, that's okay. I'll be fine."

"I don't mind. We'll spend some time together. Let me get my coat."

"Harry! I'm just going to Allison's! It's okay."

"All right. Fine. Just trying to be a nice guy."

Helen felt terrible. She touched his cheek. "I appreciate it."

Harry sniffed manfully and turned away. He could take it.

Helen cursed Bozo and Simon and all spooks everywhere. She ran up the stairs to change.

Harry grinned and entered the kitchen, picking up the phone.

Gib sat at the mixing console in the audio lab, riding a potentiometer, and wincing as he listened to sizzling, French-accented love-talk.

"No, no. Doucement. Do it slowly. Very slowly . . ."

The source of those velvety imperatives was Jean-Claude Dercle, a banking expert Sector had recruited from the University of Lyons, who stood inside a glassed-in booth, reading his lines into a stumpy Neumann microphone that picked up every subtle nuance of his Charles Boyer imitation.

"Yes, yes. That's the way, cheri . . ."

Gib's briefcase phone rang and he picked it up.

Harry's voice: "Is Jean-Claude finished yet?"

"Not quite. Harry, you've reached a new low with this one. I can't believe you're crazy enough to use the room at the Marquis."

"Why not? You think I can afford a suite like that on a public servant's salary?"

"Oh, yes! Oh, yes! Ohhhhhhhnngh!" Jean-Claude was losing himself in the part.

"Cut!" yelled Gib into the console mike. "Just stick to the script, Jean-Claude!" He spun around to the DAT recorder, cued the tape back a few seconds. Into his phone, he said, "Harry, tape'll be there in twenty minutes. Gotta go."

Sexy, sexy . . . No, not that one. How about this? Oh, God. Earth tones, earth tones, I'm so sick of earth tones! *I haven't got a thing to wear!*

Helen searched frantically, fruitlessly. A glimpse
of something black at the end of the rack. Black is
sexy! She lunged for it. Oh, God! A less sexy black
dress had never been conceived. Long chiffon
sleeves, a flounce at the neck, another at the knees.
She wouldn't get a whistle, walking through Soledad
with that on. Look at the time! Helen started to
change, then realized Harry might see her leave.
The dress was a little too uptown for a trip to the
pharmacy. She stuffed it, and some high-heel pumps,
and her small purse into the carry-all. She could
change in the garage.

The Marquis meant luxury and especially privacy,
from the first floor to the last. It hosted its share of
Washington fund-raisers, but it was better known as
a place where the staff kept their mouths shut. Even
as Helen drove her red Accord forward in the line of
limousines, inching her way toward the parking va-
lets, half-a-dozen members of Congress were *geboom-
semachen* in rooms somewhere above, and not with
their wives or husbands. Actually one of them, an
important senator, was on the couch, having his
diaper changed by a very strict mommy who thought
he was a dirty boy and needed a spanking.

In a place like this, an unescorted female, usually
wearing only a tube dress and a compensatory air of
hauteur, was pretty unremarkable. Helen, however,
caught the reception clerk's eye right away. The
pathetic pretense of dignity was there, but she de-
parted from custom first by looking like a school-
teacher on her one night out a month; second because
she was carrying a giant purse more appropriate for
a trip to the beach than an evening of elegant glamor;

and third, because she fell off her high heels, not once, but twice on the long trek across the hotel lobby.

"Do you have an envelope for Doris?" said Helen with as smoky a voice as she could manage.

The clerk arched his brows. What a preposterous name.

"Doris?"

"Yes, Doris," she said, cursing Bozo for the thousandth time that day.

"Let me check," he said, eyeing her chiffon flounce with a mixture of fascination and revulsion. He retrieved an envelope from the message box, and handed it to her.

"Thank you," she said.

"Thank *you*," he said.

She walked away, opening the envelope. Inside she found a room key, a tiny device that was probably a bug, and a slip of paper with a phone number on it. Helen veered toward a bank of phone booths, digging in the bottom of her carry-all for a quarter.

She dialed the number from the slip. Someone picked up the phone. "Listen." It was mechanical-voiced Boris. "You are a prostitute named Michelle."

No way.

"Go to room 944. A man will be there. He is a suspected arms dealer."

"Now hold on, Boris. I'm not going to let this guy . . . you know . . ."

"You won't have to. He has particular tastes. He likes to watch. You will say his regular girl, Carla, is sick. If he likes you, he will tell you what to do. Before you leave, you must plant the bug near the bedside telephone. If you do not accomplish your mission, the deal is off."

Click.

Helen exited the elevator on the ninth floor, oriented herself, and headed for her assignation. She watched the numbers on the doors . . . 940 . . . 942 . . . She stopped to tweak her hair and lipstick in a hallway mirror, and froze.

The woman who stared back at her from the mirror was not a call girl. She was an uptight Bethesda homemaker. Named Doris. Helen didn't need a tweak, she needed a total overhaul.

Makeoveeeer! her mind screamed like a battle cry. Helen reached up and tore the flounce away from her neckline. Cleavage. How's that, you jerk? she thought, addressing an imaginary arms mogul. Next she ripped off her long sleeves. Arms! As if you cared if I have arms. She stepped back, saw the flounce shrouding her knees and tore it away, exposing another nine inches of thigh. Legs! How's that, creep? Actually she was all right with guys who liked legs. It was boob men she despised. Now the hair. She grabbed a base of flowers from the table under the mirror, tipped it, catching big handfuls of water, and dousing her hair. She slicked her hair back in a chic wet look. Last, but not least, her mouth. She put on lipstick so red it looked like she'd just raised her head from a kill.

And voilà. Soledad was on fire.

Too bad it wasn't Harry in that room, she thought, absently running her thumb along her wedding band. Then the ring got her conscious attention. It had to come off. She tried. It wouldn't! It hadn't been off in years. She licked her finger, twisted it. *Owww!*

Finally, it came free. She put the band on her right
ring finger and turned the modest diamond palm-side
down, out of sight.

Ready. A deep breath. I am a slinky call girl. She
dropped the bug into her cleavage, stuck her key in
the door, and entered.

She walked into the sumptuously furnished outer
room of the suite, staring out the window at the
breathtaking Washington lights. Before her eyes
could adjust to the dim light, she heard a deep,
French-accented voice: "Hello," it said.

Helen turned and saw a seated man silhouetted
against the floor to ceiling wraparound windows of
his bedroom.

"Put down your bag," the voice purred.

Helen put her carry-all on the coffee table.

"Now have some champagne."

Helen obeyed, pouring some into a slender flute.
The room was so quiet, the fizzing wine seemed
loud. She turned to face the man. Sipped. Oh my,
there was nothing better.

"Come in here," he rumbled, with just a hint
of menace.

She walked toward the bedroom.

"Step into the light."

A slash of moonlight came through the windows
beside her. She walked into it, revealing herself
to him.

"My name is Michelle. Carla's sick. She thought
you might like me, so—"

"Shhhhh," said the voice.

It was Harry of course, and his hand, out of sight
behind the chair arm, held a tiny DAT tape deck.
He thumbed the pause button, and Jean-Claude's

voice murmured: "Let me do the talking. You are very pretty. You may start by unzipping your dress."

I may, may I? She reached back and started to yank the zipper down.

"No, no. *Doucement*. Do it slowly. Very slowly."

Slime. Helen turned her back to him and very slowly, languorously, revealed her creamy back to him.

How's that, Froggie? Bet you wish you could touch it.

"Goood," the voice moaned. "Now slip the dress off, slowly."

Yeah, yeah, *doucement*, douche bag. Helen looked over her shoulder and gave him a contemptuous look, then slipped the dress off her shoulders, excruciatingly slowly. She was getting into it, working the guy up. She tried to think of it as torture. She let the dress slide down her body to the floor. She stepped out of the little black puddle, turned and stood there, hand on hip, legs apart, wearing high heels, a black thong, and a lacy bra.

Harry was literally starting to tremble. He had planned on giving his wife a taste of something dangerous and illicit, but he was about to start howling and take a big bite himself. Oh baby! You're hurting me! In his mind he was whimpering like a dog. He felt like the wolf in a Tex Avery cartoon; except it wasn't his eyes telescoping. He couldn't have stood up if he wanted to. He thumbed the DAT deck, desperate to move on.

"Now slide the nylons off one by one," said the oleaginous voice.

Helen looked puzzled. "I'm not wearing any." He liked to watch—except he was blind.

Harry quickly unpaused the next line.

"That's good. Now the bra."

Oh, God. Helen hesitated, furious, then turned her back to him and unhooked her bra, slowly stripping it from her body. Whoops. The bug fell out and rolled under the canopy bed. Oh shit! She froze.

"Now turn, cheri. In the moonlight. Let your body flow like water."

I'm naked in front of a pervert! How did this happen! her mind shrieked. Helen felt like she was losing control. But she mustn't! She steeled herself and turned to face him. Okay, that wasn't so bad. At least he didn't make any funny noises or start abusing himself. All right, Pepe Le Peu, I'll flow. I'll flow right over to that bug and stick it up your phone.

She let her body go, slinking toward the canopy bed, leaning suggestively against one of the corner posts.

Harry panted in the shadows, staring at her lovely skin, like blue milk in the moonlight. She was looking at down at him like she owned him. Amazing. She could do this for another man. It didn't make him angry somehow. He didn't care. He was there. All he could think about was her. She was so beautiful. So tough. He wished he could just drop the recorder and eat her alive. But he was stuck. She'd kill him if she found out. What a stupid idea!

But when this is over, I can race home. And she'll be there. And then . . . Harry heard a bestial roar deep in the center of his mind. Harry suddenly wanted to fast forward the tape, but he might land in the middle of a cue. He had to take it step by step. Damn! He thumbed the pause button.

"Now dance for me," was the silky command.

"Go on." Well, maybe this wasn't such a bad idea after all.

Helen saw her chance to get the bug. She grasped the corner post with both hands and conjured up a beat in her mind, bumping and grinding, writhing and undulating. . . .

Where'd she learn to do *that*? wondered Harry.

Helen slid down, down, then reached for the tiny silver gleam under the corner of the bed. She lost her grip on the bedpost and fell backward, but rolled onto her stomach and splayed her legs, like a pinup on a polar bear rug. It almost looked like she planned it. She rolled around a bit, did a slinky leopard-crawl toward the bed, and and grabbed hold of the corner post again, quickly retrieving the bug before she pulled herself up. She slowly straightened, turning her back to him, and popped the bug in her mouth.

Harry had no idea what the hell was motivating all this, but he didn't want it to stop. Still, he had to get them out of there. And hoooome! He thumbed the pause button.

"Let your hands be a lover's hands on your own skin as you move," said the velvety voice. Oh, God. Harry hoped he could stand it.

Helen, with her back to him, began to caress herself, modestly at first, then more suggestively.

Harry thumbed the button. He couldn't remember what the next line was, but he hoped it was "Turn around!"

But Jean-Claude was apparently satisfied. "Yes, that's it," he moaned. Damn.

But then Helen did turn. Oh, my God, thought Harry, about to explode. It felt like his entire groin was caught in a bear trap. I've got to get out of here, he thought. Last line, please, he released the pause button.

"Now, lie on the bed and close your eyes."

Helen completed the rhyme: And then I'll give you a big surprise. This was dicey. She could see he was large and broad-shouldered. But somehow she wasn't afraid of this guy. She sat herself down on the bed, lay back, and closed her eyes almost all the way.

Now was Harry's chance. Leave some money on the bedside table and sneak out. Then she'll hide the bug, and they'll both go drive hoooome!

Except she was so utterly sexy and beautiful. Harry did something foolish. He took a rose from the table vase beside him and walked over to the bed. He sat down just behind Helen's head. Her eyes fluttered, but stayed closed. She was breathing quickly. So was he. He stroked her hair. Then he touched the petals of the rose to her eyes, caressed them, then her soft cheeks, then her lips. Her lips . . .

For Helen, trusting a stranger like this, naked and vulnerable, and his being so gentle . . . it was indescribable.

And then the disgusting pig kissed her on the lips. Helen flung her arm out, grabbed the telephone off the nightstand, and brained him as hard as she could.

"Get off me, you scum!"

"Owww!" screamed a suddenly much-less-French voice. He covered his head. She bounced the phone off his skull again, sending him to his knees.

Helen rolled off the bed and ran around gathering her clothes, dressing herself as fast as she could.

The big jerk was down on all fours in the middle of the room, holding his bleeding head and moaning. He tried to get up. Helen booted him in the ribs.

"Ooof!"

She zipped up her dress, running into the other room for her purse. She scooped it up and—stopped in her tracks. The bug! She took it out of her mouth and ran back into the bedroom.

The pervert was trying to get up again. She gave him another kick.

"Owww!"

She crawled across the bed, stuck the bug under the shelf of the night table, then scrambled for the door again.

"Jerk!" she yelled as she passed the moaning man.

"Helen," Harry's voice croaked. "Helen."

She stopped dead in her tracks. Turned slowly.

"Harry?"

Harry rose painfully to a kneeling position, holding his head. "I know it looks bad, but I can explain."

But Helen's mind was in gridlock.

"Harry—?"

Craaack!

The door lock to the adjoining suite shattered, and two men wielding machine pistols burst into the bedroom. Harry recognized them as workers from Juno Skinner's warehouse.

"Get your hands up! Up high, now!"

Craaack! The front door. Two more armed men ran in from the outer room.

Harry got to his feet, hands in the air. He would not resist with Helen there.

Oh, my God, poor Harry, Helen thought. "He's got nothing to do with this," she said. "It's me you want."

"Quiet, Helen," Harry barked. He turned to the

man he pegged as the squad leader. "Let the hooker
go. She's not important. You don't need her."

Helen cut him off. "Harry, please. Just let me
handle this."

The squad leader shoved Harry toward his wife.
"Shut up, both of you."

His men handcuffed Harry, searched Helen's
purse, then pushed them toward the door. Helen
twisted around to talk to the leader. "Listen, you
don't need him. He's nothing. He's a sales rep for a
computer company—"

The squad leader cuffed her across the head.

Helen looked shocked.

"Well, that was unnecessary," she said as he
propelled her out.

Minutes later, they emerged from an emergency
stairwell onto the hotel's loading dock. A rental van
waited, engine, running and door open.

The gunmen pushed Harry and Helen inside, then
followed them in. The door slammed and the van
sped away.

Helen and Harry huddled together behind the
driver's seat, staring at four very hairy and unfriendly
faces hovering over the barrels of four bellicose-
looking machine pistols.

Helen tried to understand what had happened to
her. The biggest conundrum was Harry.

"What were you doing there?" she asked.

"You wouldn't believe me," he said. He seemed
different to her. He was stony, utterly calm, as if
being pushed around by armed foreign agents actually *relaxed* him.

"Harry, you've got to—"

The squad leader jammed his pistol muzzle against her cheek. "Talk again and I'll kill you."

Harry imagined the man's death so vividly, that it leapt from one mind to the other, and the squad leader saw it. His eyes widened in fear, but only Harry noticed.

Harry leaned back and closed his eyes, resting and gathering himself for what was to come. The Crimson Jihad had captured him. But they had made a very big mistake. They hadn't killed him.

Eight

Aziz received word: Renquist was captured. Good. Aziz had use for him now. It was clear he wasn't some CIA hack who had stumbled onto their plans. He'd been identified as the man who caused the debacle at Khaled's chateau. That incident, and his performance during the mall rub-out attempt reinforced Aziz's belief that Renquist was one of Washington's most special field agents, almost certainly assigned to nuclear containment.

Aziz's men had tailed one of the surveillance teams watching Juno's offices, following them back at the end of a watch to a nondescript office building, then into a front company called Tektel Systems. That was as far as they got. Then one of the Tektel surveillance people drove from Juno's to the Marquis Hotel and delivered something to a suite on the ninth floor. The next day, one of Aziz's men posed as room service and knocked on the door. Renquist's burly partner answered. After that, they set up a watch.

To the extent that Aziz was a zealot, he would have liked to empty an AK-47 into Renquist, then pull the pin on the four MIRVs right in the middle of Washington, D.C. But his anger had to be controlled, like everything else. The MIRVs were priceless commodities. He would use them to buy something equally priceless. Freedom. And Renquist would play a small but important part in Aziz's plan to turn the United States into a pitiable, helpless giant.

And after he had served his purpose, cruel, subtle Samir, perhaps the world's preeminent torture, would ferry the American across the river Styx to a very special Hell that was waiting for him.

The turbines on the G-3 jet whined up to speed, screaming louder and louder as it taxied out of its private hangar at Baltimore-Washington International.

The Jihad's rental van screeched to a stop next to the hangar doors. Harry and Helen were shoved out, Harry still handcuffed.

A long, black limousine slid up, stopping beside the van. Akbar, the driver, got out of the car. It took him a long time, and not because he was slow. He was the mountain that Muhammad had moved. He opened the back door and a pair of long, lovely legs came out—a hard act to follow, but the rest of Juno Skinner did so, and very well.

Helen gaped: the gleaming private jet, the terrorists, the limousine, the femme fatale. She looked around for Roger Moore.

Then Juno . . . moved . . . toward Harry, her almond eyes sparkling with wry amusement.

"Hello, Harry," she said.

Helen would never forget what happened next.

"Juno," her husband said. "I wish I could say it was a pleasure to see you again."

Helen's jaw actually dropped open. *"You know her?"* she blurted.

Harry pretended he didn't hear.

"Who's your little friend?" Juno asked, giving Helen a dismissive glance.

What a bitch! "I'm Helen Tasker," she said, looking Juno up and down. "Harry is my *husband*. And you are . . . ?"

"I'm Juno Skinner," said Juno, turning to run her eyes over Harry. "And Harry is my favorite dancing partner."

Helen turned ominously to Harry, who rolled his eyes.

Juno nodded to the squad leader. The martyrs goaded Harry and Helen toward the jet's cabin door.

Helen walked down the aisle of the luxuriously appointed jet. *Very* nice. The quality of the people kidnapping her was rising steadily. If this particular group of maniacs killed her, she would at least have the consolation of expiring on real leather, instead of in Simon's smell factory on top of a combination tablecloth/bedspread.

Akbar, the man-mountain, pushed Harry and Helen down on a plushly upholstered banquette extending under the windows behind the cockpit. He strapped them in.

As Akbar bent over him, Harry noticed something in the giant's beard: a few lucky grains of couscous clung there desperately, having escaped the fate of

millions of others being torn apart inside the man's
volcanic gut.

"There's enough food hanging in your beard to
feed a family of four," said Harry disgustedly. "Why
don't you go clean yourself up?"

Akbar cinched Harry's lap belt tighter than necessary.

"Look, Harry's not part of this," said Helen to
Juno. "He's just a sales rep."

Juno laughed. The woman really seemed to believe
what she was saying. She was kind of funny, really.
"No, my dear. He is a federal agent. He killed two of
my colleagues the other night."

"You don't understand," said Helen, frustrated.
"We've been married for fifteen years—"

Harry kicked his wife's heel to shut her up.

Juno, intrigued, shot a puzzled, speculative glance
at Harry.

Harry sighed, disgusted. "Look, Juno, this is just
some whacko hooker I met in a bar."

Helen was furious. "Harry, what's the matter with
you? Tell them the truth." She turned to Juno.
"We're married, we have a daughter—"

Harry cut her off again. "I don't know what this
crazy bitch is on, but you should just cut her loose
so we can get down to business."

But Juno just chuckled, enjoying the show.

"I'm not going anywhere!" said Helen. She turned
to Juno. "Look in this locket! Go ahead! I can prove
it!" Helen pointed at her chest with her nose.

"Great," muttered Harry.

Juno leaned across, took Helen's locket in her
hands, and popped it open.

Awww. There they were. Daddy Bear, Mommy

Bear, and Baby Bear. All sporting eight-dollar hair cuts. Juno almost retched.

"How sweet, she said to Harry.

Harry just stared at her coldly.

Juno waved a flight attendant over, then turned to Helen. "Something before we take off?"

The attendant whipped a pneumatic injector off her tray and pressed it against Helen's bare shoulder. *Hissss!*

'Owwww! That hurt! You biii— Helen slumped sideways onto Harry's shoulder, falling unconscious.

Juno stared at Harry, curious. "She was telling the truth, wasn't she, Harry? She really doesn't know How interesting."

Harry just looked at Juno, or pretended to. Actually he was looking out the window behind her. keeping track of their position and direction From his training flights, he knew they were taxiing onto a runway designated for southbound private and commercial jets.

Juno nodded at the attendant again, who leaned over and ripped Harry's sleeve down at the shoulder A cold metal touch. *Hisss.* Harry settled himself in a comfortable position, trying to guard against soreness or pinched nerves from what might be hours of forced unconsciousness. The barbiturate spread from his veins, into his heart, and rushed up to his brain. Harry felt himself drop suddenly into that murmuring stream of condensed images that under pins all conscious thought, the place where all stories are born.

When Harry had a problem to solve, he would wake in the dark of early morning and put a metal marble in his hand. Then, with his arm off the edge of the bed. he would direct his thoughts, eventually drifting away. back toward sleep, and fall into that preconscious stream His mind showed him things then pictures voices. stories. told him jokes. often showing him a solution to his problem along the way And before he went fully unconscious. the marble would slip from his fingers and bang on the floor, waking him. allowing him time to cement what he'd seen into consciousness Then he would drift off again. marble in hand

In the seconds before he fell unconscious on the banquette. Harry dipped into that stream He saw the bearded faces of his captors. men of warm climes They wouldn't like cold and messy winter storms . . . He saw a wallowing ship plowing toward the semitropical south, toward the crowded coastal corridor of the United States   And last of all—and Harry hoped he didn't smile before his pilot light winked out—he saw Gib. sitting in a warm pool of light, sewing a tiny tracking transceiver into Helen's purse The purse that was lying right beside Harry on the plane.

The G-3 landed in southern Florida. at a private airstrip built during the Reagan era as a jumping-off point for smuggling arms to the Nicaraguan Contras Now it was supposedly abandoned; but for an abandoned airstrip in the middle of the Everglades it was looking pretty good No palmetto roots were tearing at the tarmac No alligators basked and yawned on the warm runway Somebody was taking pretty good care of it. probably drug-runners Which was convenient for the Crimson Jihad. who needed to transfer two drugged captives to an Aerospatiale helicopter for further transport south.

Akbar exited the jet, shouldering Harry like a sack of yams. Another man carried Helen. Man and wife were thrown, still unconscious, into the back of the A-Star. Akbar and the gunmen got in behind them. Juno got in the front. The A-Star took off immediately, skimming the mangrove swamps, heading southwest into a reddening sky.

During World War II, Navy Seabees put up hundreds of way stations on islands in the Caribbean and in the Keys of South Florida; depots where airmen and seamen could refuel and repair their crafts. The island depots were part of the preparation for a coastal defense of the United States, which could become necessary if Axis strength kept growing and Nazi battleships crossed the Atlantic, or if the German U-boats tried to blockade U.S. ports.

They were still there, jerry-built, corrugated tin facilities, with creosoted timber wharfs, weathering slowly in the tropic sun and storms; lonely, modest monuments to our national readiness during dark days when people still feared war might come to our shores.

And now finally it had. And ironically, it was one of these very facilities, on an islet the locals called Noname Key, that sheltered the Crimson Jihad. Or rather it was infested with them; a noble memorial to American courage defiled by their hatred, their murderous purpose, and their mustaches.

Just before midnight, a small freighter of West African registry hove to off the coral and limestone islet. Two motor launches, acting as tenders, brought the ship alongside the aging pier Next to the pier was a two-story warehouse of corrugated metal

No one would have taken too much interest in a freighter anchored there. Beat-up tramp steamers docked at these depots often enough, using them to make repairs, or as makeshift trading posts. But the dozen powerful floodlights were very unusual, and so was the activity they illuminated: Over thirty armed men with bushy black mustaches swarmed over the dock, carrying cargo, food, and fuel between the ship, the warehouse, and three U-Rent trucks parked in an adjacent clearing.

Standing guards kept watch at the edges of the mangrove swamp behind the compound, and more on the jungle road leading through the swamp.

Aziz himself supervised the unloading of the four most precious pieces of cargo A rusting, old gantry crane lifted one of the fifteen-foot-long, tarp-swaddled objects from the hold, then trundled it to the warehouse

The rhythmic sound of a chopper's rotors faded up suddenly. Aziz and his men cocked weapons, ready for friend or foe The Aerospatiale rocketed into sight, low over the water, coming around the back of the key The copter wheeled and settled over the clearing, landing beside the three trucks.

Juno stepped out of the A-Star's front door The sliding door in the back opened and the rectangular Akbar stepped out, looking more like cargo than a passenger He pulled Harry, groggy and hooded, out of the copter and held him up with one hand. Helen staggered out next, held up by Akbar's other tree-trunk arm. She was also hooded.

Akbar turned both his captives so that they faced

his commander, then pulled them up to attention. Aziz strode over and pulled their hoods off.

Harry immediately swiveled his head, taking in every detail of his surroundings. Then he settled his eyes on Aziz.

The two stared at each other with utter, naked hatred. Each killed the other in a dozen humiliating ways during those few seconds they held eye contact But oddly enough, they had a lot in common with reunited lovers. They had each longed to see the other again; they were overjoyed to have found each other; and each had exciting plans for the other's future. Except that future could be counted in seconds, maybe minutes, at best, hours.

"Who is this woman?" Aziz asked.

"His wife," said Juno.

Aziz, in a perverse parody of Harry's recent consciousness-raising, saw not a wife, but a wealth of possibilities.

"Good," he mused. "Bring them."

Aziz led his entourage into the floodlit warehouse. winding his way through dozens of packing cases lying open on the cracked concrete floor The crates were full of assault rifles, ammo clips, grenade launchers, and all the other matériel necessary to equip the Crimson Jihad's small army.

But the stars of the show were four huge stone figures lined up side by side in the middle of the warehouse. Aziz walked up to them and stopped

The ancient figures. features blurred by centuries of scouring wind, were Sphinx-like warrior horse men: winged stallions from whose bodies grew the torsos and heads of bearded, armored men.

Harry didn't need X-ray eyes to know what was inside them.

"Incredible, aren't they?" said Juno. "Warrior figures from the Persian Empire of Darius the First, around 500 B.C. I call them the Four Horseman of the Apocalypse."

Harry felt sick. As a reward for her utterly psychotic witticism, Harry moved her up three places on his shit list—a list no one stayed on very long.

Aziz nodded to a man wearing safety goggles. The man swung up a jackhammer, stepped forward next to Juno, and blasted away at the body of the nearest horseman. Stone fragments flew, then chunks fell away revealing a dark cavity inside the body of the figure. A coffin-shaped metal container nestled inside.

The jackhammer trimmed away at precision-cut shelving that supported the metal box above and below. Four men came forward and slid the box out of its niche, then lowered it carefully to the floor.

Aziz stepped forward. A hush fell over the group. "Open it," said Aziz.

The four men flipped up latches at each corner. They lifted the lid and carried it aside.

Inside the case lay a conical object, about five feet long. Yellow-tipped like candy corn.

Aziz signaled Akbar, who thrust out one of his giant arms. Harry found himself stumbling forward toward the warhead.

"Do you know what this is?" asked Aziz.

Harry gave the object a knowing stare and nodded. "I know what this is. This is an espresso machine." He looked at Aziz, checking to see if he'd won the

prize He tried again. "It s a snow cone maker"
Wrong answer A water heater?'

Aziz lunged and grabbed Helen by her hair, pulling her toward him. He whipped out a dagger and
pressed the point under her chin, forcing her head
back The point punctured her skin

Helen gasped

Aziz hissed in her ear Do you know why you
have been brought here?'

"N-no, she said She couldn t quite seem to keep
her head back far enough—

Aziz enlightened her· 'So that this man can verify
to the world that Crimson Jihad is a nuclear power"

"How can he do that?' she muttered through
clenched teeth careful not to move her jaw 'He s a
computer salesman, for chrissakes'

'If we are wrong about him. said Aziz coldly,
"then the last thing you see will be your blood
spraying in his face. ' He jerked her head back even
farther and pressed harder with the dagger Blood
ran freely down the groove and over his hand.

Helen s blood. I'm gonna think up something really
good for this guy. Harry promised himself. He walked
up close to the conical object and examined it.

'This is a Soviet MIRV-Six he said, 'from an
SS-22N launch vehicle. The warhead contains 14.5
kilos of enriched uranium, with a plutonium trigger
The nominal yield is thirty kilotons Then in fluent
Arabic. Harry said. 'Release her and I'll cooperate'

Aziz pulled the knife away from Helen's neck and
tossed her aside as if she d ceased to exist He
barked an order to his men, and they went to work
extracting the other three MIRVs

Helen just stared at Harry, her mouth open in horror.

Harry shrugged. 'What can I say? I'm a spy.'

She walked right up to him, stared in his face, curious and cold. The man who had shared her bed for over fifteen years was a complete stranger.

'You bastard.' She reared back and punched him full out, right in the face. *"You lying son of a bitch!'*

Aziz signaled for two of his men to handcuff her before she seriously hurt Renquist. He needed the man in one piece. For a little while anyway. Aziz spat with disgust. If a Sunni woman had done that she'd be well, he'd forgotten the penalty for hitting your husband, but he knew it was something gruesome

And look. the big ox was miserable.

"I'm sorry, honey,' Harry said, knowing nothing he could say could ever make up for what she'd just learned.

"Don't call me honey!" Helen screamed. 'You don't ever get to call me honey again! You under stand?! You pig!'

Juno laughed. This was too funny.

Helen wept, appalled and betrayed. She turned to the gunman holding her purse. "Give me a tissue!'

Akbar took her purse from the soldier and rum maged. But Juno took one out of her own purse "Here you go, dear,' she said, dabbing at Helen's eyes. Helen didn't thank her.

Akbar, a highly professional and very thorough sort of a pituitary case, gave the purse a once-over, checking the lining as a matter of course. He felt something in the bottom. He ripped open the stitching and pulled out the GPS transceiver

"Commander!" he cried 'Look at this!'

Aziz strode over snatched the tracker in a trembling hand, then threw it on the floor. and smashed it with his heel

"You bugged me?" screamed Helen at Harry

But it was Aziz who was most enraged He spun on the men who had captured Harry and Helen. screamed at them in Arabic They each fell to their knees, trembling and begging forgiveness Aziz pulled out his handgun and shot each of them in the head.

Helen hid her face, horrified

But Harry was trying not to smile The Crimson Jihad's first five martyrs were not exactly covered in glory It was bad enough that they'd overlooked the transmitter in the first place But Aziz had put another nail in their coffin. The smart thing would have been to transport the beeper to. say. Boca Raton Or put it on a jet out of Miami But smashing it here was like sticking a pin in the mapscreens at Omega Sector

Aziz turned to Harry, controlling himself. seeing Harry's barely concealed delight Aziz looked at his watch "It's too late to stop me pig. I promise you"

He began barking orders in Arabic and his men scattered chanting exhortations to one another

Akbar walked over and accosted Aziz. 'Commander."

"What is it?"

With his broad back turned to Harry and Helen Akbar showed Aziz something else taken from Helen's purse a wallet-sized picture of Dana

"Good work. Akbar I won't forget. Go Call our people in Washington"

* * *

Faisil was watching the tracking screen when the locator signal winked out 'We've lost the signal.'' he announced

He and Gib, and several other Sector agents were flying south at supersonic speeds. working inside the agency's Citation jet, a mobile tactical command center

Gib hurried forward from the communications ter minal

'Son of a bitch! Where?'' he said

Faisil pointed to a tiny dot twenty miles west and south of Marathon, and just north of the Overseas Highway

''One of the Keys. There's no name listed.'

Gib started sweating bullets. Aziz must have found the transmitter He'd be pissed, and he seemed like a pretty self-indulgent kind of guy. Even if he had some use for Harry and Helen, he'd be hurrying now to get it over with and then dispose of them.

Gib leaned into the cockpit. "How we doin'?"

'Miami TCA, said the pilot, pointing at a glitter ing metropolis below We're on a final. Better take your seat.''

Gib went back to his communications terminal and got on the horn.

'Cav One to Miami, DEA. over.'

'Copy, Cav One.''

''You guys got those choppers flight ready? I want to take off the second we land.''

"Pilots report two green machines, sir, over. Ro tors are spinning.'

Gib signed off and scanned a mental check list There was nothing more he could do till they landed Shit! He needed something to do A big bag of pork

rinds would be real handy right now. Gib strapped
himself in, his guts in a knot. Jesus, he thought,
about to start crying. He had to face it. The two
people he loved most in the world were probably
dead.

Abdel Mubarak liked to watch American TV. He
had been reprimanded many times for missing a
weapons drill, or a call to prayer because they came
in the middle of a rerun of *Happy Days* or *Taxi*. But
tonight his weakness had actually been rewarded
when his squad leader handed him a half-inch cam-
corder, a videotape, and an operating manual, and
told him to get ready to record the commander's
message to the world. Abdel was now the Crimson
Jihad's Official Videographer.

Except that at this moment he really, really wished
he wasn't. His sweating eye was steaming up the
eyepiece as he nervously, surreptitiously checked
focus on Harry, wondering if he was framing too
tightly—what was that he'd read about overscan? His
face was hurting because like all novice camera
operators, he was squinting so fiercely if there'd
been a zit on the left side of his face it would have
exploded. Worse, he was starting to get the shakes.
The weight of this tremendous responsibility was
making Abdel tremble.

Harry, meanwhile, spoke directly into camera,
wondering if the swaying, skinny man with the
nervously bobbing Adam's apple would last through
his entire speech. And I hope he doesn't have a zit
on the left side of his face, thought Harry. But what
he said was: ". . . and I can verify that they have the
arming box and all equipment necessary to detonate

the four warheads. This is absolutely the real thing, people."

Abdel watched the image in his eyepiece carefully, saw Harry stare at him, saying nothing. Then Harry rolled his eyes and nodded his head to the left Abdel felt someone jab him in the kidneys and remem bered—he swung over to bug-eyed Aziz who stood in front of a crowd of Jihad warriors looking very eager to tell the citizens of the United States that he had them by the short and curlies.

"You have killed our women and children." he began, finding himself trembling as he thought of his parents, "Bombed our cities from afar like cowards And you *dare* to call *us* terrorists."

It was then that Abdel, the Crimson cameraman, almost fainted. A battery shape with a diagonal slash started flashing in his viewfinder He struggled to remain conscious, felt sweat instantly pour out of his head and down his neck . . .

"But now." Aziz continued, "the Oppressed have been given a mighty Sword to strike back at their enemies. Unless the United States pulls all military forces out of the Persian Gulf area, immediately and forever, Crimson Jihad will rain down fire on one major U.S. city each week until these demands are met."

Aziz was fulfilled, on a roll It was all coming true. a dream he had nurtured consciously or uncon sciously, since he was fourteen

But for Abdel this was a nightmare The low battery warning was flashing more and more rapidly Oh, Allah, be merciful! What should I do?

Aziz stared into the camera, right into the eyes of his enemies "First one weapon will be detonated on this uninhabited island as a demonstration of Crimson Jihad's power and our willingness to be humanitarian. However, if these demands are not—"

Abdel's viewfinder winked out and he lowered the camera, trembling, ashen-faced.

Aziz's eyes almost popped out of his head.

"B-b-battery, Commander," said Abdel.

"Get another one, you moron!"

Abdel handed off his camera and hurried to comply. Aziz rubbed his temples, wondering if this was what they meant by a migraine. His warriors shifted from one nuclear-powered foot to another.

Harry started whistling "Edelweiss." Aziz's enraged look cut him off. Aziz turned to Juno.

"Take them to Samir. I'm finished with them."

Escorted by two Crimson warriors, Juno led Harry and Helen inside a filthy, crumbling cinder-block building near the edge of the swamp. Its rotting walls were lit by naked bulbs encircled by a cloud of desperate, doomed bugs.

Two steel chairs were bolted to the floor facing each other. The gunmen sat Harry and Helen in them, then one of them stepped back and leveled his weapon, while the other unlocked and relocked their handcuffs so that they were shackled to the chair backs.

Then Samir entered. He was a stooped, spectral man, completely hairless, dried up, and mahogany-colored, like an unearthed mummy. He shuffled into the room, carrying a sort of doctor's satchel, breathing rapidly and shallowly. Emphysema, thought Harry. Samir put the bag on the table and opened it, taking out his tools: needle probes and scalpels, specula, clamps, drills, Dremel tools with saw blades . . .

"This is Samir," said Juno. "Can you guess his specialty?"

"Oral hygiene?" asked Harry.

"What's going on, Harry?" blurted Helen. She knew as well as anyone what was about to happen, but she found herself wanting to get Harry's attention away from that *slut*, Juno. Why wasn't she sweating?! And what exactly was the *purpose* served by walking around with your big boobs popping out all over the place?

Juno turned to Helen and said, "Samir is going to ask Harry some questions. See, we're not even sure which agency Harry works for. Now, Samir is absolutely first-class, but on the other hand we have Harry here who has managed to lie convincingly to the woman he loves for fifteen years. So it will be interesting to see how long he can resist."

"This will help," said Samir. He held up a syringe and squirted a little of its contents into the air, then tapped out the bubbles. He knew what he was talking about. He'd learned his trade from Nikolai Gordievsky—the man the KGB called The Truth. And Samir was a worthy pupil—in great demand in certain circles for his uncanny ability to put together just the right mix of serums and tortures to break any individual combination of body type and temperament. He was a rich man by now, and only took jobs that interested him. This was one. He was honored to play a role on so diverting an occasion as the first enemy detonation of a thermonuclear device on U.S. soil.

Samir injected Harry's muscular arm with a serum he'd prepared just for him.

Helen winced as the needle went into her husband.

"You know, you really should swab that with alcohol," suggested Harry. "I might get an infection."

Samir smiled. He had teeth like a mummy, too.

"I'll return when this has taken effect," he said. "Then we'll talk."

"I'm looking forward to it," said Harry, oddly sincere.

Helen closed her eyes as Samir walked past, expecting to get an injection, too, but Samir just walked right by.

When she opened her eyes, her husband was looking over her head at that cow, Juno.

"Why are you helping these raving psychotics?" Harry asked.

"Because they're very well funded raving psychotics," Juno replied. "And I'm getting a lot of money." She moved up beside Helen, looking down at her, seeing how much Helen hated her.

Juno took another step and knelt between Harry's legs, stroking his thighs. "You think I care about their cause?" she said. "Or yours?" She looked at Harry with amusement, like he was a relic, passé. "America is on top now. But so was Rome once. All civilizations crumble. One nation succeeding over another . . . What does it mean in the long run?" More stroking. "The only important thing is to live well. And living well takes money."

Harry had never seen anything so beautiful look so repulsive. His face showed the pity of it.

"You're damaged goods, lady," he said. He felt his

words slur a little and realized that Samir's drugs were coming on.

Juno stood up. Disrespect was bad enough, but pity—Who the hell are you to pity me? She turned and looked at Helen with an evil glint in her eye.

"Did you tell her about us, Harry?" she said.

Harry ceased to feel sorry for her. "There is no use, you psychotic bitch."

Juno wanted to tear out his eyes, but she bit her lip and went for something more hurtful.

"Sure, say that now," she purred. She bent over him, kissed him passionately and long on the mouth. She straightened and looked over at Helen, savoring the look on Helen's face. She turned once more to Harry and said, "Thanks for everything, Harry. You were . . . one of the best I ever had."

She strode over to the nearest Jihad warrior and plucked a grenade from his webbing. Then she knelt in front of Helen and wedged the grenade between wifey's knees. She pushed Helen's knees together, making sure they held the spoon against the side of the grenade. Then she pulled the pin.

"Now just keep your knees together and you'll be fine."

Helen sneered. "You wouldn't last very long in this situation, would you?"

"Owww! Hold that thought," said Juno, walking away. "Watch them," she said to one of the martyrs, and walked out escorted by the other.

Helen carefully crossed her ankles, giving herself more leverage on the grenade. Then she looked up at her husband.

A wave of euphoria broke gently inside Harry.

Wow, man. He was starting to feel like an easy-going kind of a guy. Sensitive, honest, pacific . . .

"There was nothing," he said. "I swear."

"That's worth a lot after lying through your teeth for fifteen years." You wouldn't have known it from the anger in her voice, but Helen desperately wanted to believe him.

Harry's head slumped forward on his chest. He grinned at something. He's obviously drugged, Helen thought, and the guy said it was truth serum. "What did they give you?" she asked.

"Sodium amytal. Maybe some other truth agents." Harry found that funny, too.

"It makes you tell the truth?"

"Yes," he said distractedly, watching the bugs, his mouth hanging open.

"Is it working yet?" Helen asked.

"Ask me a question I would normally lie to," he slurred helpfully.

"Are we going to die?"

"Yup," he answered, and lit up the room with his grin.

"I'd say it's working," said Helen.

Harry sighed, feeling real good: "Yeah, I'd say they'll either torture us to death, shoot us in the head, or leave us until the bomb goes off."

"Okay, okay. I get the picture." Helen realized that she could open Harry up like a ripe fruit. Few wives ever got an opportunity like this. Go for it, girl.

"How long have you been a spy, Harry?"

"Seventeen years."

"My God." She still couldn't believe it. "Have you ever killed anybody?"

"Yeah," said Harry, "but they were all *bad*."

She remembered all the long days, the overseas trips . . .

"Have you had to have sex with other women in the line of duty?"

"I don't take those assignments," he said, matter-of-factly.

"What about Juno?"

"Oooh, she's really a fox isn't she?" he said with an amazed grin.

Helen considered opening her knees, but thought better of it when she realized she wouldn't get to *see* him die.

"Did you pork her, Harry?"

"No," he said factually, then felt compelled to add, "but I wanted to."

Helen felt like crying. In fact she felt so much like crying that she went ahead and did it, staring right in her husband's face.

"Are you a total, lying, scum-sucking pig, Harry?" she sobbed.

Harry, with infinite tenderness, said, "Looks that way."

Then Samir returned and, without even glancing at his prisoners, went to his table and began selecting and arranging his tools.

Helen pulled herself together. Harry took a deep breath.

"Are you ready to begin?" asked Samir with that hackneyed facetiousness that seems to afflict so many torturers.

"I wouldn't come over here if I were you," said Harry gently.

"And why not," asked Samir, pausing in his work.

"Because I've got a really big fart on board just waiting for you."

This was a new one for Samir. He blinked like an owl. Allah Akbar, it was truth serum after all.

Then Harry broke into a boyish grin. "Just pulling your leg. No, the real reason is I'm going to kill you."

Samir breathed a sigh of relief, as if that threat were infinitely preferable to the other.

"I see," he said indulgently. "And how will you do that?"

"Well, I thought I'd break your neck, then use your body as a shield, then kill the guard with that knife there on the table."

Samir turned and walked toward Harry, a long steel needle probe in his hand. "And what makes you think you can do all that?"

Harry pulled his hands out from behind his back. The handcuffs hung off his left wrist. "I picked the lock on these handcuffs," said Harry.

He exploded out of his chair, grabbed Samir's bald head and twisted, cracking his neck like a twig. Harry took two steps to the table and swept up the knife.

The shocked guard hadn't even leveled his weapon when the knife shattered the socket of his left eye and buried itself in his brain.

Helen watched the guard crumple to the floor, barely two seconds after Samir had fallen. She stared in shock. Harry?

Harry stripped the fallen guard of his 9mm machine pistol and slung it on. Then he walked over to Helen and knelt in front of her.

"Don't move," he said. She nodded, still looking at him in awe.

Harry slipped his hand between her thighs, then his other hand. He slid them toward her knees, surrounding the grenade, sliding his palm down over the spoon. Then he froze.

"What is it?" she asked, alarmed.

"God! You've got great legs."

He's still shit-faced, she realized.

"Harry. Snap out of it!" God. Husbands are so helpless.

Harry went back to work, lifting the grenade out.

"Got it, baby," he said. "Give me an earring."

Helen obeyed, removing a simple silver hoop from her ear. Harry took it and forced the silver ring into the pin slot, disarming the grenade.

Then he went around behind her. He twisted one of the oversized knobs on his DiveMaster watch, then pulled, unsheathing a tiny lock pick. He went to work on Helen's handcuffs.

Moments later they emerged from the tiny building and scurried to the edge of the mangroves. Harry stopped there, squatting in the shadows, scanning the dock and warehouse area.

Helen leaned up against him. "Tell me something before this stuff wears off and you start lying again."

"What?" said Harry.

"Do you still love me?"

"Yes."

"As much as you used to?"

"No," said Harry truthfully, looking straight into her eyes and breaking her heart. "Much, much more."

Harry made a friend.

"It wore off," said Helen, grinning.

Yells came from the torture building.

"They found the bodies," said Harry. "Come on."

He grabbed her hand and ran along the edge of the swamp, toward the palm forest. A light flashed across them, someone cried out, then the light found them again. Two terrorists sprinted toward them, opening up with AK-47s.

Harry veered into the palms, trunks splintering from bullet rounds as he and Helen disappeared into the bush.

Like most people, the warriors of the Crimson Jihad were disinclined to enter dark jungles where desperate killers lurked. Calling out nervously for backup, the two men stepped into the palm forest, behaving more like prey than predators.

Which is what they were. Harry lunged at them without sound, streaking from the shadows. He yanked one man's rifle away, and swung it at the other, knocking that man's AK into the trees. The first man whipped out a combat knife and swiped at Harry, but fear made his arm swing too far. Harry stepped in and grabbed the man's wrist, shoving the blade into the man's partner. The guy tried to pull his wrist free, but he could have chinned himself on Harry's arm. Harry smashed the man with his left elbow, then dropped the confiscated AK on the ground and took the man's head in his hands and—

Helen, behind a nearby palm, covered her ears—

Snap!

Helen hurried to his side. "That's so disgusting, Harry. Can't you just shoot people like everyone else?"

"I don't like to leave a mess."

Two more martyrs came hurtling through the bush toward them. Flashlights waved. Arabic yells. Harry looked down at the AK lying across a log near his feet. He stomped on it and it flipped into the air. Harry caught it in a firing position and peppered both terrorists in the chest with short, well-aimed bursts. Then he scanned the bush, game face on, looking like a feral animal.

Helen couldn't quite believe what she was seeing. His shirt hung in tatters across his muscular torso; he was scratched and bleeding and holding an assault rifle.

"I married Rambo," she muttered.

Harry turned and kissed her.

"I *crap* higher than Rambo," he said.

He took her hand and pulled her away, heading back into Aziz's maw.

A guard with a MAC-10 slung across his shoulder patrolled the catwalk high above the warehouse floor.

He eyed the area by the doors, where a dozen of Aziz's men loaded one of the U-Rent trucks with conventional weapons from the open crates. He watched several shoulder-launched Stinger antiaircraft missiles go on board, hoping someday he'd get a chance to fire one at his father-in-law.

But the main event was shaping up in the very center of the warehouse. The gantry crane lowered one of the warheads into a shallow pit jackhammered out of the concrete floor and the long dead coral underneath. A half dozen men attended the MIRV's deposition, watched over by an impatient Aziz.

The guard on the catwalk was thrilled. This warhead, they all knew, was going to definitely go off. God is great! That would be a sight! He was lost in the glory of it all, so he didn't turn to look behind him, down the flight of steep, metal stairs that ran up to his perch. The stairs that Harry Tasker silently climbed, followed closely by his wife.

Harry snuck up behind the man, took his head in both hands—

Oh God! Helen covered her ears.

Crack.

Harry grabbed the man's MAC-10 before it could clatter to the floor.

Helen sighed. Is that *really* necessary, she wondered.

Harry bent close to her ear for a little wife-torture. "It's funny. Everybody's neck sounds different."

She winced. They heard sudden loud yells from below. Helen grabbed Harry's arm, alarmed.

"They're calling for quiet," he reassured her.

Harry pulled her toward the edge of the railing, and they peered down at the warehouse floor. Aziz stood in front of the pit, all his men gathering in a group in front of him. He began a passionate speech in Arabic. He pulled a chain from around his neck, selected a metal arming key, one of four, then raised it above his head, declaiming to his warriors.

Harry translated: "In ninety minutes a pillar of holy fire will rise at this place as a sign to our enemies."

Aziz jumped down into the pit, stuck the key into the warhead's arming computer, then turned to look at his followers. He turned the key.

On the warhead's computer, a LCD timer counted down from 89:59.

"It is done!" Aziz shouted. His men roared their approval. Two men pulled Aziz out of the pit, and two others tipped a concrete mixer, deluging the warhead in quick-drying cement, filling the pit.

Aziz continued his harangue.

"What's he saying?" whispered Helen.

Harry looked bored. "Now no man can stop us. We are set on our course. No force can stop us. We're cool, we're badass, blah, blah."

A last rhetorical flourish from Aziz, and a bellicose cheer full of fury and triumph rang out below. The terrorists all began firing automatic weapons at the ceiling.

Harry pulled Helen under his wing as ricochets clattered off the beams, scattering all over the inside of the building.

Aziz waved his arms and shouted out an order. Another cheer and the warriors of the Crimson Jihad went back to work at double time.

Harry peered back over the railing. The U-Rent with the conventional weapons drove back to the clearing. The two other trucks backed into the doorway with their trailers open. Forklifts slid two of the remaining warheads into them. A third forklift trundled slowly past, carrying the fourth and last warhead toward the Aerospatiale.

Helen was puzzled: "If we're on an island, why are they using trucks?"

"We must be in the Florida Keys," said Harry. "The Overseas Highway connects the islands to the mainland."

"So there's no border, no customs. There's nothing to stop them."

"Just us," said Harry, cocking the MAC-10, and flipping off the safety.

"What are you going to do?" asked Helen with

dismay. She realized that somehow, these relatively idyllic few moments on the catwalk had been their second honeymoon.

"I'm going to go down there and kill everybody, I guess," said Harry.

He handed Helen the MAC-10. "Oh shit," she said.

"Wait here. If you have to use this, use it. Don't choke, okay?"

Helen nodded gamely. Harry ran down the stairs to the warehouse below. Helen saw him slip behind a packing crate, undetected.

Harry reached into his pocket, took out Juno's grenade, and pulled the earring. He threw the grenade as hard as he could, bouncing it off the wall at the other end of the building.

Kablooom!

The blast deafened the warriors in the warehouse, echoing back and forth within the tin walls. The localized carnage—a buffet of finger foods and a couple of snacking terrorists were now mixed in a ragout—was minor compared to the confusion created by the noise.

Harry used the distraction to move out. Except there was someone behind him—someone cursing in surprise and raising an AK-47.

Harry sprinted for cover, tripped on an air hose running to a jackhammer, and went sprawling, losing his AK-47 under a pallet piled with heavy equipment. Uh-oh. A quick peek: Seven warriors of the Crimson Jihad converged on him; weapons raised.

Harry looked up to Heaven as if in supplication and yelled, "Shoooot!"

Helen obeyed. *Brrrrrraaat!* She flew backward from

the recoil, but wasted two of the warriors before slamming into a metal brace and braining herself. The MAC-10 fell from her hands and tumbled down the stairs, crashing hard on its clip—*Brrrrat!* The wild burst killed two more of Islam's finest. The gun somersaulted and smashed its butt on another metal step—*Brrrraat!* Two more terrorists felt bullets hit their chests, and shock waves burst their hearts.

The last terrorist desperately skidded to a halt, everything going in slow motion. In half a second, he would have his momentum stopped and be diving out of the way. His feet scrabbled for purchase. The MAC-10 cartwheeled toward the last step, spinning, the barrel coming around . . . The terrorist saw his martyrdom coming—*Smash* went the clip—*Braat!* went the gun.

"Aaaargh!" went the martyr.

Harry peeked out from behind his cover and saw all seven attackers lying stone dead. Damn. He looked up at Helen and waved. She waved back. Out on the warehouse floor, the warriors began yelling, pointing at the catwalk. Helen had been spotted.

"Run! Outside! Hide!" yelled Harry; and she did, as bullets sprayed the metal grating all around her.

She hurtled to the end of the catwalk and through a doorway, onto an exterior stairwell. The last Harry saw of her, she was closing the door as bullets ripped into it, pimpling the metal.

Harry turned his attention back to the warehouse floor. He had to get to those nukes. He ran forward, maybe two steps. A guy as big as a house rose up out of nowhere and smashed Harry in the jaw. Harry rocked back, then forward; another punch knocked him backward. He tripped over the air hose again and fell on his ass.

The big guy leaned over one of Helen's victims, picked up the dead man's AK-47 by the barrel, and strode toward Harry, planning to beat him to death.

Harry grabbed the air hose and reeled it in, dragging a jackhammer into his lap. He lunged upward and said hello to the big man—*Brat-tat-tat!* The jackhammer shattered the man's sternum and made mud pies out of his guts. Harry let him keep the jackhammer, but grabbed the AK-47 as the man fell backward.

More Jihad warriors raced toward Harry, firing their weapons. Harry couldn't afford to retreat. He waded into them, swiveling his gun as each new threat presented itself, slaughtering Aziz's men, inexorably moving toward the trucks with their warheads inside.

Aziz caught glimpses of Harry across the warehouse, advancing through the crates, emptying his weapon into his men, then picking up another from a dead man, striding forward. Aziz cursed him.

He turned and shouted to the drivers of the trucks. "Go, go! Wait for us down the road!"

The trucks started up.

Harry saw the trucks pull out. He broke off his advance, running for a side door on his right, banging through it.

The trucks sped through the clearing, heading for the jungle road beyond. Harry ran outside and raked the trucks with his AK, keeping his finger on the trigger. The doorway behind Harry erupted with gunfire.

Harry ducked and sprinted toward the front of the warehouse, chased by crisscrossing tracks of exploding tarmac. He dodged behind a tanker truck parked at the front corner of the warehouse.

Oh shit, thought Harry. FLAMMABLE LIQUID, it said, right in front of his face. He was hiding behind a tank full of aviation fuel and there were very upset Crimson warriors running toward him from the dock, and more from the side of the warehouse, and they were firing guns.

On the bright side, he noticed Helen waving desperately from behind a forklift in the clearing.

That's a relief, thought Harry, as he unhooked the tanker's nozzle, cranked open the valve, and released a torrent of av-fuel. He laid his AK's muzzle right across the mouth of the gushing hose and fired. The muzzle flash ignited the fuel, and voilà, Terrorist Flambé.

The first to get it were the guys racing at him from the doorway at the side. Then the guys running from the dock. They were almost seventy feet away when the fireball hit them and they felt their mustaches burn away. Screaming like banshees, they stumbled blindly toward the water, never making it.

Like any demon from Hell, Harry looked best in firelight. He painted the dock and the front of the warehouse with roiling flame, setting people and vehicles on fire, scattering horrified warriors. Then he toasted the dock.

He turned his attention to the clearing where the Aerospatiale and conventional arms truck sat parked. Aziz was there, standing beside the truck, and he had a LAW rocket on his shoulder aimed right at Harry.

Oh shit. Feet don't fail me now.

Harry sprinted away from the truck as hard as he could, heading for the dock thirty feet away.

No one in the clearing could see Harry running for the water, but it wouldn't have mattered anyway. He'd never make it. The rocket *whooshed* out of Aziz's launcher, an unsteady trail of smoke tracing the missile's flat, very brief flight into the center of the tanker.

Kabooooom!

The gas truck exploded in a giant fireball.

Harry hit the black water just as a bright orange sheet of fire passed over him.

Helen had her hands over her mouth, watching the burning wreckage of the gas truck. "Oh, my God. Harry."

He was dead. She was just getting to know him.

A pistol pushed against her temple. A manicured thumb cocked the hammer.

"My condolences to the widow," said Juno.

Helen turned and stared at her Other. Cruel, shallow, bitch. Helen wound up and slapped her as hard as she could. The blow left a bloody slash across Juno's cheek.

Juno felt wetness, reached up to her cheek, and brought her fingers away covered in blood. She grabbed Helen's hand and turned it over: The diamond on Helen's wedding band was still turned palm side down.

Juno's face darkened. "You messed up my *face!*"

she screamed. She brought her pistol up and pressed it against Helen's forehead.

'Bye, wifey. Juno pulled the trigger.

"No!" barked Aziz, knocking her arm into the air. The bullet arced into the sky. "We may need a hostage."

If looks could kill, both women would've died right then. Juno reluctantly backed down. And Helen enjoyed every second of her slow compliance.

Lights flashed through the palm forest, coming from the road. Warriors cried out and cocked weapons.

Akbar spoke up. "It's mam'sel's limousine, Commander."

"Good. Take this woman with you," said Aziz, indicating Helen. He turned to Juno. "See that she comes to no harm." He walked away toward the A-Star.

Juno pushed Helen toward the arriving limo. "Let's go, Suzy Homemaker."

Nine

Harry fought panic and the urge to inhale as he kicked and pulled, keeping his rhythm, trying to get beyond the edge of the inferno. One stroke at a time. Another. Still brightness above . . . then blessed blackness. Harry kicked and pulled upward, bursting into the cool night air, gasping and gulping down oxygen.

He spun around, treading water, scanning the dock and clearing. Through the fire and smoke he caught sight of Helen. Juno was prodding her along with a pistol. Akbar opened the rear door of a long black limousine, and Juno shoved Helen inside.

Aziz stood by the Aerospatiale, barking orders. A half dozen of his men loaded the fourth warhead into the copter's rear compartment, getting in behind it. The turbines on the helicopter wound up to takeoff speed. Aziz jumped into the front; the doors closed. The pilot pulled pitch, and the helicopter lurched into the sky, its rotors fanning the flames beneath. It pulled north and east, quickly picking up speed.

Harry backstroked as the rotor wash fanned the flaming slick toward him. He struck out around the edges of the flames, heading for shore. There were maybe seventy-five minutes left before the nuke detonated. Running seven-minute miles, he'd be ten miles down the road when it blew. He might survive the blast, but the radiation would kill him a few days later.

Gib, you better get your ass down here fast.

Akbar followed the U-Rent trucks down the jungle road to the Overseas Highway. His headlights briefly flashed across the scattering, tiny forms of some Key deer, miniature creatures that over the years had migrated down the highway from the mainland. Too bad for them, thought Akbar, they would be hamburger in about an hour—or as Akbar pronounced it, "hambooger."

He accelerated up the onramp and onto the highway, letting the trucks set the pace. Miami 110, said the sign. Ninety minutes away. He'd be watching the little deer turn to plasma in his rearview.

A thundering roar passed overhead, penetrating the limousine's soundproofing. It was the Aerospatiale hurtling toward Miami at 150 knots, hugging the deck as if weighed down by its Luciferian cargo.

The highway stretched over the ocean as far as Akbar could see. A pale, gray edge of the coming dawn lined the ocean ahead and to his right. He dimly recalled a fragment of a song almost a thousand years old:

*Awake! for Morning in the Bowl of Night has flung
the Stone that puts the Stars to Flight . . .*

This dawn, the Crimson Jihad hurled their own
bright stone, a stone as bright as any Sun.

Akbar had forgotten what he'd learned as a child:
that the poet/astronomer who wrote those words
spent his days in a garden of love, and his nights
looking at the stars. And that he despised all men
of violence.

Gib looked out the door of his descending Bell 206
helicopter at the southeastern end of Noname Key.
Shit, Harry's been doing some landscaping.

It was definitely what they meant by an "after-
math." The rotors whipped thick columns of smoke
off chunks of burning wreckage. There was no single
thing that he could see that had not been riddled
with bullets, blackened by fire, or demolished by an
explosion. He peered around through the smoke.
Charred bodies lay everywhere, though none looked
big enough to be Harry. Please God, don't let me find
him like that.

The copter landed and Gib and the other agents
jumped down. Gib was dressed for battle, swiveling
an AR-15 along with his eyes. He double-timed
through the shambles, eyes flickering over every
corpse he passed. Not a sign of life anywhere. Gib
started to get a tight feeling in his chest and forced
himself not to yell Harry's name.

And then out of the swirling smoke by the dock,
backlit by a saffron dawn, there he was. Dripping
wet, ripped up, bleeding, and walking like a juggernaut straight toward Gib.

"Harry!" Gib forgot his commando training and

ran toward his friend, grinning like an idiot. "I thought this looked like your work!"

Harry walked right past him.

"Let's go. I'll brief you in the air."

Uh-oh. Game face. *Total* game face.

Harry and Gib had no time to enjoy the kaleidoscope of pink, green, and blue coral flashing by below. As the Bell 206 hurtled down the causeway, they bent over mobile com-units, working feverishly.

They and several other Omega agents jabbered into their headsets, mobilizing federal, state, and local forces for an evacuation of all the Keys between Marathon and Big Pine. Everybody talked at once; the energy in the copter controlled, but very high.

"You tell the sonofabitch this is a Bright Boy Alert," Gib hissed. The White House chief of staff didn't want to get out of bed. "Repeat, Bright Boy Alert. And I need a patch to the White House ASAP. . . . That's right. Get 'em both up, now!"

This was the day they had all been trained for, but none of them were happy it had finally come.

Harry spoke to the commander of Patrick Air Force Base: "The Coast Guard needs thirty minutes to motor out to a twenty-mile radius. That gives them half an hour for pickup. They're going to miss people, and those people will need an airlift . . . I'd say a Bell on every Key between Marathon and Pine, ASAP."

Gib, having completed another call, whipped around to Harry. "Two Marine Corps Harriers will be here in twelve minutes. Out of Boca Chica."

"Good," Harry said, putting his hand over his headset mike. "I'll brief them on the way in."

"Handing off to you. Line five. I've got to talk to the cops in Miami." Gib punched at his dial pad, setting up a conference call to the police chief and head of the FBI field office in Miami.

Extrapolating out, Gib figured the nuke heading for Miami was in fact their most serious problem. By his reckoning, the A-Star would be approaching Miami airspace any second now. There would be no one even remotely prepared to deal with it. The two men Gib was rousting out of bed were about to wake to a nightmare.

Akbar wished he had a nice black shot of coffee right about now. The fat, orange sun of early morning was right in his eyes and making him sleepy. The highway was boring and empty this early, and he didn't even have the trucks for company, because Juno, just in case there was trouble, had ordered him to hang back a mile. Cruise control was on, set at the legal limit. Everything was conspiring to make him doze off. It felt like the edges of his eyelids were magnetized. He decided to ogle the females in his rearview mirror.

Juno rested her 9mm handgun in her lap, pointed in Helen's direction. She silently cursed Aziz for saddling her with this tedious babysitting job. She was tired, too, and needed a drink. Luckily, that's one thing she could have. She opened the sunroof first, letting the cool morning air bluster in and refresh her. Then she opened the fridge and pulled out champagne and orange juice.

"Mimosa?" she asked Helen.

"Fuck you," was the steely reply. Helen watched

Juno smile her catty smile and sip her refreshing cocktail.

Drink up, you twat. I'll just sit here and figure out a way to outsmart you.

Gib ran down the basics to a local police captain on a Key outside the blast area.

"Just get your patrol cars out—all right, your patrol *car* out—and go through the streets with your P.A. on telling everybody to stay away from their windows, and don't look at the blast . . . Yeah—" Gib heard a crescendoing roar.

"Here they come," said Harry.

Out the open door of the Bell, Gib saw them: two hunch-winged V.S.T.O.L. Harrier jets passed the Bell at 500 knots, tracking along the causeway toward the mainland.

"Roger, Mike Three Five, you are cleared to engage," said Harry to the wing leader. He wished he was with them, instead of on this big, clumsy, lettuce chopper. "Be advised, your targets have Stingers and light machine guns."

The pilot of the lead Harrier said, "Copy that, Bright Boy One. Tally-ho."

Gib marveled, as always, at flyboys' total dissociation from reality. They'd *scream* by, sitting inside hurtling engines of destruction that looked like giant, psychotic insects, heading for a sky full of smart missiles and cannon fire, and you'd hear a voice over the radio say, with trancelike calm, "Tally-ho." They had to be on drugs.

First, the Harriers jetted away from the highway, out over the water. Then each pilot took a deep breath and held it as they punched into a tight turn. They strained mightily, forcing up their blood pressure, pushing back against the G-forces that might black them out. They flattened out and streaked for the causeway, racing the sound waves that would tip their arrival.

A Jihad lookout on the lead truck, which was loaded with conventional arms, noticed the two jets streaking toward his flank and sounded the alarm, relaying the news by walkie to the other vehicles.

Too late. The first run was a strafe. 25mm cannon shells and rocket pods ripped parallel lines in the ocean and shattered the highway tarmac, ripping through the second truck in line, which was carrying a MIRV. The truck exploded into a skeletal flaming wreck before it smashed through the guard rail and doused itself in the green water seventy feet below.

But the young warrior-lookout in the lead truck had a Stinger missile ready as the Harriers banked for another run.

He stood on the sill of his window, elbows braced atop the cab of the truck, waiting as the jets screamed directly toward him. He let the missile go.

The Stinger shot upward toward the lead Harrier. The wing leader banked and turned, juked every way a jet could juke. The Stinger almost clipped his wing. They pulled out of the run.

"No joy, no joy," reported the wing leader.

Harry had watched that sortie unfold through his binoculars. He had some advice: "Mike Three Five, recommend you use your Mavericks to take out the bridge."

The wing leader came on: "The Mavericks are packing H.E., Bright Boy One. Won't set off the nukes, will they?"

"Negative. That's a negative, Mike Three Five." Harry turned to Gib, off mike, and said, "Probably not, anyway."

One Harrier came in low; the other arrowed down from on high. Each fired two Mavericks and pulled out, well before they were in range of the Stinger missiles that were waiting for them.

The Mavericks finished the trip, racing straight at the span just ahead of the speeding trucks. They shattered the support trestles, the roadway, and the lead truck in a quadruple explosion. The entire span crumbled into the water.

The driver of the remaining truck stood on his brakes, hoping there was enough road, screaming for mercy from the Almighty. The Crimson warrior riding shotgun also had his leg extended, pushing just as hard on the imaginary brake his mind had conjured as some kind of last pathetic fantasy of control over one's fate.

But the roadway ran out, and their front wheels dribbled over the edge . . . then miraculously, they stopped, literally teetering on the brink.

The two men in the cab held their breath, afraid to move . . . the truck teetered forward. The martyrs in the back, locked in the trailer with the MIRV, clamored for information.

"Don't move!" screamed the driver. "I'll kill you if even breathe!"

The truck started to settle back, slowly but surely. The driver almost wept with happiness.

Then a pelican, belly full from its morning feed, and needing a little rest, alighted on the front of the truck and stood there like a pot-bellied hood ornament. The truck groaned, and ever so slowly, tipped forward.

"Get off! Get off!" the driver shrieked, but the bird only stared at him with that permanent prebelch look that all pelicans have. The driver pulled out his sidearm and fired desperately through the windshield. *Blam Blam Blam!* The hollow point slugs turned the pelican into a blizzard of feathers. But it was too late.

"Aaaaaaaah!" screamed the driver.

"Aaaaaaagh!" screamed his partner.

"Aaaaaaaagh!" screamed the men in the trailer.

They slid off the edge and plunged seventy feet onto the unmerciful concrete wreckage of the bridge. Then they blew up.

"Good shooting, Mike Three Five," said Harry. "Stand by on station."

"Roger, Bright Boy One."

Harry turned his attention to the limousine, coming up fast, and streaking down the highway toward the precipice. There was no way a driver would see the missing span in time, not with all the smoke and going that fast.

Harry turned and ran into the back of the copter. "Gib!" he yelled.

Akbar repeatedly keyed his walkie-talkie. "Come in, Hakim! Come in, Assar!" A mile ahead, the black smoke of fuel fires dirtied the blue sky.

Juno looked ahead, too, wishing Akbar would stop yelling. She had been right to stay back.

But she had been wrong to take her eyes off Helen.

Helen lunged at Juno, grabbing her gun, wrestling with her on the seat behind Akbar. Juno fired wildly as they struggled, her arm flailing back and forth, the gunshots deafening in the tiny, enclosed space.

Akbar winced at the noise, punched "resume" on his cruise control and twisted around to help Juno, keeping one meaty hand on the wheel. Just as he turned, Juno's gun jabbed into his eye socket and went off, splattering the sun visor and windshield with his brains. Akbar slumped against the door, no longer the chauffeur.

But his giant, dead leg pressed the pedal to the metal.

"Oh, my God!" screamed Juno. "You stupid bitch!"

Helen ignored the no-driver problem and concentrated on the gun. They fought like Titans, hitting and slapping and tearing and rending.

The limousine tracked lazily toward the guard rail and smashed into it, throwing up sheets of sparks. Juno used the jolt to help her push Helen back, and they both rose up off the seat, their hands locked high over their heads, sticking out the sunroof. Helen banged Juno's hand against the edge of the sunroof and the pistol went flying out of the car.

The car hit the guard rail on the other side and they both tumbled onto the seat again, Helen on top. Helen grabbed Juno by the hair and smashed her head against anything hard, the phone, the counter-top, the cup holder. She reached for the champagne bottle, about to brain her, when she saw something terrifying out of the corner of her eye.

A quarter mile away, the highway came to an end.

Juno saw it, too. "Oh, my God!" screamed, clambering into the front seat. She pulled and tugged at the man-mountain, but he was like a bag of cement. She threw her leg over him, trying to squeeze it under the steering wheel, and down onto the brake . . . There was no way.

Helen heard the *Thackathacka* sound of a helicopter and looked up through the sun roof. She couldn't believe what she saw.

Harry. He was alive. And he was reaching for her from the skid of a Bell 206 descending toward the limo.

"Harry!" she screamed with happiness, climbing on the backseat and reaching out from the sunroof.

Harry hooked one arm and a leg over the skid and hung down as low as he could.

Gib hung out the door of the Bell, giving hand signals to the pilot, and screaming, "Lower! Lower!"

The copter pilot was freaking. If his skid caught that limo at this speed, they'd tip and pinwheel into the drink. He inched lower anyway, but the ground-effect wind whistling over the limo pushed him higher. He dipped into it again, feeling the skid drag in the high-speed current along the top of the car.

Harry strained down. Helen strained up. Their fingers met and clasped—*Smash!*—the limo hit the guard rail. The force jarred Helen loose, throwing her to the other side of the sunroof. The limo caromed off the rail and slid across the highway.

Gib directed the copter pilot. "Get over the car!"

Juno pulled with all her might on Akbar. He fell

over between her legs, his face pressed against her belly, pinning her to the seat. Juno looked out the windshield and saw the end of the world a second away.

Harry reached out as far as he could.

"Come on, Helen! Come on!" he yelled.

Harry locked hands with Helen and pulled her out of the sunroof just as the limo arced out into space, carrying Akbar, Juno, and Juno's scream toward the concrete and water below.

The Bell sailed out over the water, then circled back toward the causeway.

"I got you, baby, don't worry! I got you!" yelled Harry.

Helen and Harry looked at each other, ecstatic with joy and relief and love—her looking up, hanging a hundred feet over the ocean locked in her husband's life grip; him looking down from the skid of a helicopter, fiercely holding on to the thing he loved most in the world. It was an odd place to discover that you were truly, now and forever, perfect soul mates. They grinned at each other, eyes locked as tightly as their hands.

The two Harriers floated down onto the causeway next to the wrecked bridge span. Their engines shrieked hellishly. They bounced on their big wheels and settled.

Behind them, Harry's Bell 206 was already down, and the other was descending.

Harry checked his watch and nodded to Gib. "Any second now," he warned.

Gib brought up his bullhorn. "Showtime, folks. Don't look at the flash. Do not look at the flash."

Helen looked nervously toward the southwest, then at her husband. Harry put his arms around her.

"We're safe here," he said drinking in her face. Helen reached up and stroked his cheek—the diamond—Harry took her hand and turned it over. He slid the ring off her right hand and slipped it back onto its rightful finger. They embraced and their lips met in a deep and loving kiss.

And behind them the sky lit with unholy light, a blasphemous, soundless echo of that first Crack of Light, the One Hand that clapped at the dawn of time.

And they kept kissing, eyes closed.

A bright balloon of atomized matter jelled, then a roiling cloud formed and levitated toward the stratosphere, pushed upward by a thundering column of electrified smoke.

And they kept kissing. Then they felt waves and waves of radiant heat and pulled apart to smile at each other. Helen would have stared at him a while longer, but Harry's curiosity got the better of his sentimental side. He turned to look.

The sound hit them then, the dull thud-crack. For all the biblical majesty of the spectacle, Harry felt himself shuddering. Buckminster Fuller was probably right: The nearest human beings should get to a thermonuclear reaction is 93,000,000 miles away.

As the mushroom cloud began to spread and drift off with the trade winds, Gib got some bad news over his headset. "Roger, that," he said, and waved Harry over—urgently.

Harry saw and turned to give Helen an apologetic look.

"Go to work, honey," she said.

Dream wife, thought Harry and strode off toward Gib.

The Harrier pilots—wondering who the filthy, torn-up lubber with the Priority One Command Clearance was—looked at her curiously.

"That's my husband," she said, describing his most important claim to fame.

Over by the Bell, Gib took Harry by the arm and pulled him away from any possible eavesdroppers. Gib took a deep breath and gathered his thoughts before speaking: He had to make sure Harry had all the information he needed before he went ballistic.

"Okay." He was ready. "Aziz's copter landed twenty minutes ago in Miami. He's on the top of a high-rise downtown. SWAT's on the scene, and I got the cops sealing off the area. He rendezvous'd there with about a dozen more faction members, and they're barricaded on the twentieth floor." Now came the ballistic part. "They have a hostage. It's Dana."

Harry felt a cold sweat break out all over his body. He almost vomited.

"*My* Dana?"

"They grabbed her during the night from my house, took out two of our agents. I'm sorry, Harry. I thought I had it covered—"

But Harry was already gone, sprinting toward the nearest Harrier.

Gib ran after him. "Harry! We'll get her out! We have a man inside already! Harry—!" He was wasting his breath and he knew it. "Shit! *Here we go.*"

Harry strode right past young Captain T. R. Hut-

cherson of the United States Marines. "I need to
borrow this thing for a few minutes, Captain," said
Harry, climbing the ladder without waiting for a
reply.

Hutcherson gaped. The guy had Clearance One,
but he was a mess. His clothes looked like Bruce
Banner's after he turned into the Hulk. And anyway,
thought Hutcherson, this is *my* sled. "Sir? Excuse
me! . . ."

Gib got right in Hutcherson's face, his mood as
ugly as any drill sergeant's. "Force Comm told you
Clearance One, am I right, mister?"

"Yessir, but . . ."

"No buts or it's *your* butt. That's coming right
from the President, Captain."

"Yes, sir!"

Gib turned and scrambled up the ladder to the
cockpit. Harry settled himself in.

"I'd like to remind you," whispered Gib, "that it
has been ten years since you were actually in one
of these."

"If I break it, they can take it out of my pay," said
Harry, strapping on his webbing.

"Thirty-three-million-dollar replacement cost,
Harry. That's 733 years of total garnishment. I suggest you come back in one piece." Gib handed Harry
an Omega rover. "Take this in case we need to talk."

Harry gave his friend the closest thing to a smile
that ever came out of his game face, then returned
his attention to the controls, trying to remember
what each one was.

Gib closed the canopy and climbed down, silently
wishing Harry luck. He was going to need it.

Harry put his left hand on the throttle levers,

grabbed the stick between his legs, and worked the rudder pedals with his feet. The vector control lever next to the throttle was still set for vertical. He checked the toggle switch for the gas turbine: on. Igniters: on and ready. He eased the throttle forward. Fuel flowed into the main engine and ignited; the engine turned over, winding up from a roar to a scream to the signature Harrier shriek.

Meanwhile, Gib's fantasies about icy-calm Marine pilots were going down the drain. They were hopping around like they had to pee, screaming at Harry.

"Do your one-finger checks! Check your duct pressure!" yelled Hutcherson.

"Check your flaps! Your nozzle settings!" yelled the other pilot.

But Harry couldn't hear a word. He looked out and saw the jet pilots hopping around and waving at him. He waved back. Then he saw Helen, looking worried. He winked at her, then pushed the throttle further forward. A gigantic howl filled the air.

The Harrier lurched upward to the full extension of its landing gear, straining to get up.

Gib stood with the pilots, watching in horror. Hutcherson looked like he was going to weep.

"It'll be fine," lied Gib. "He's got hundreds of hours in Harriers. Joint ops, cross-training, all that stuff."

The big plane wobbled off the ground like a drunken bumblebee, 23,000 pounds of thrust ripping at the pavement and throwing up debris.

"He's a little rusty," admitted Gib. "But it's like riding a bicycle . . . you never forget . . ."

The Harrier drifted alarmingly sideways, directly toward them.

Gib started backing away, faster and faster. "Uh—Seek shelter!"

They ducked and scattered as the jet slid right over them, only six feet off the ground. The wheels clipped the light bar off a police car.

Luckily, Harry started getting the hang of things just about then, firing the puffers under his wings, nose, and tail, getting his balance. He looked out at a squatting, terrified cop outside and mouthed "Sorry," then gave it full throttle and lifted straight into the sky.

At fifty feet he steadied, pulled in his wheels, and spun on his axis, pointing the nose north.

Gib sighed explosively, straightening up beside a worried Helen.

"He's got it," said Gib, like there was never a doubt.

Harry's voice came over the rover on Gib's belt.

"Gib, you copy, over?"

Gib brought the rover up: "I'm here, buddy."

"Tell Helen what's going on. Tell her I love her. And ask the pilot where the button for the 25mm cannon is."

Gib turned Hutcherson to ask—*Budda-Budda-Budda-Budda!* A burst of cannon fire from above.

"Never mind," said Harry, "I found it."

He pushed the vector lever. The thrust nozzles beneath his wings rotated back. His jet shot forward, rocketing toward Miami.

Awake!

Icy, heartless fingers of dread gripped the hearts of every person in the city. Terror and panic erupted everywhere. Acts of desperation, mental breakdowns, heart attacks. Before they'd even had a chance to brush their teeth, two million people had watched a mushroom cloud soar up into the sky in the ocean south of them. Then they'd watched Aziz's televised warning, over and over. By 7:30 A.M. those same two million knew Ground Zero was downtown Miami, and they were all in their cars, all heading north, all leaning on their horns, and they still hadn't brushed their teeth.

It was Judgment Day. Nobody was ready. And everybody had bad breath.

Aziz and a dozen Jihad warriors bristling with weapons watched a large-screen television showing the worried face of a local TV announcer:

". . . This is apparently the same group which detonated a nuclear bomb south of Marathon Key thirty minutes ago."

The image cut to a circling, aerial view of an unfinished high-rise in the center of Miami's financial district. Aziz's Aerospatiale sat on top of the building, its rotors spinning lazily. Three of his men stood on the roof, waving their weapons, and firing them jubilantly into the air.

The image shrunk to a window beside the head of the newscaster. "As you can see from this live picture, several of the terrorists are firing their guns in the air." Duh! As with most newscasters, his profession had completely destroyed his brain.

Click. Aziz held the remote, and he was grazing.

Another newscast: This one showed a dashing newscaster with his sleeves rolled up, crouching inside another circling news copter. Shouting over the helicopter's engine, he said, "FBI sources tell me there are at least a dozen terrorists on the twentieth floor, and several more on the topmost, twenty-first floor of this—the as yet unfinished—Madonna Building—" *Click.*

The next channel was broadcasting the tape Aziz had made on Noname Key. Aziz's face stared out, threatening: ". . . Crimson Jihad will rain fire on one major city each week until these demands are met—"

Click. Aziz turned off the television and handed the remote to Abdel, his audiovisual specialist. He wondered if he should arrange a live satellite hookup and plead Islam's case on Geraldo. He had already fielded several calls from Hollywood superagents. . . . Geraldo would be tough on him, though. . . . Shit! He should have been prepared for this! This building was now the headquarters of the most powerful media magnet on the planet. He looked around. It was an unlikely spot from which to command the attention of the world—both floors under construction, just big empty spaces with 360 degrees of windows, but it gave the Crimson warriors a clear view of the city and the airspace around them.

And the city a clear view of them.

Aziz, followed by his three personal guards, walked to the stairwell. Warriors stationed there fired an extended burst down toward the floor below, keeping the SWAT team honest. Aziz bounded upstairs.

On the twenty-first floor, the fourth warhead lay, still and quiet inside its green metal coffin.

Dana stared at it. She stood against the wall, puffy and red-eyed from crying. Except she wasn't crying anymore. She still didn't know what was happening—two really hunky guys got killed at Gib's house, trying to protect her, then some creeps chloroformed her and flew her here, and then she saw her dad on TV talking about a nuclear bomb—it was like a bad dream. But she knew by now that it was real. And she knew that the thing in front of her was another nuclear bomb—which was a little too fucking real. And the brutal indifference of that cold iron warhead was helping Dana rediscover her bad attitude. She was starting to spoil for trouble.

Aziz walked up to the bomb and took a chain from around his neck.

Dana raised her hand: "Ahem. I have to go to the bathroom," she said.

They ignored her.

She tried again. "Excuse me . . . ?" She froze as Aziz inserted his key into the arming box of the warhead. Uh-oh.

Aziz set the timer for 0000:00. He pulled his hand away slowly, letting the chain down gently so it wouldn't jar the key.

Dana got the picture: instant ignition. He had only to turn that key. Oh. My. God.

Brrrat! Brrrrat! Aziz and his men spun around at the sound of gunfire and yelling from below. They leveled their weapons and fanned out around the stairwell. They heard a voice, two floors down, yelling: "Hold your fire! We have the news crew you requested!"

"Send them!" ordered one of the warriors below.

Down on the nineteenth floor, the Miami-Dade SWAT team parted to let an action news reporter and cameraman pass up the stairs. The two newsmen gingerly made their way up to the twentieth floor. A dozen hairy men bristling with grenades, AKs, M-

60s and gas masks stared at them like they were
unclean pork.

A pair of rough hands patted down the reporter,
then another warrior barked an Arabic command at
him. But it was the gun barrel stuck into his kidney
that the newsman understood. He climbed the stairs
toward the twenty-first floor, smoothing his hair and
tie. Next it was the cameraman's turn.

It was Abdel the Videographer doing the body
searches. He had quickly volunteered for this duty
just so he could get a close look at a real live ENG
cameraman. And he looked Persian! Almost a bro'!

But he was not, in fact, a real live ENG cameraman. He was Fast Faisil, agent of Omega Sector.
And he was right where he wanted to be: in the shit.

Aziz took a few rapid, hyperventilating breaths,
did some running in place—jacking himself up: He
needed to be on for his message to the Americans.
They saw in all anti-American Arabs what well-fed
swine most fear: fanatics on the edge of violent
lunacy; people who don't worry about food and toys
and comfort; people who will die for ideals. He'd give
them a show. He bugged out his eyes, slung a
sawed-off AK over his shoulder, and signaled for the
cameraman to roll.

"This is a communique from Crimson Jihad," he
began. "You have seen our power demonstrated. You
have seen the Holy Fire with your own eyes. Do not
force us to destroy this city. And do not try to use
force against us. I can trigger this bomb instantly.
All I have to do is turn that key . . ." He pointed
dramatically at the warhead. ". . . And two million
of your people will die!"

The reporter holding the microphone glanced nervously at the bomb, then turned to Fast Faisil.

"Can we get a close shot of the key, please," he asked. He turned to Aziz again. "Where is it?"

Aziz pointed again. "Right there—!"

Aziz didn't have to fake bugged-out eyes anymore. The key. Was gone.

"*Someone has stolen the key!*" he shrieked. He spun around wildly, his face going purple with rage.

Dana had almost backed all the way to the roof-access stairs when Aziz spotted her. She ran.

"Shoot her!" he screamed.

Aziz unslung his AK and opened fire.

Bullets chased Dana through the doorway into the stairwell, but she made it and ran up the stairs.

Dana ran out on the roof, the chain and arming key flapping from her hand. She looked around. What a nice day. The weather *sucked* in D.C. Shit! There were creeps with guns over by that helicopter, but they hadn't spotted her. She ran the other way, over to the rooftop's construction crane.

She looked upward. She definitely felt like getting farther away. She stuffed the key in her pocket and started climbing, moving around to the side of the crane flush with the edge of the roof. If the Jihad creep shot her off the crane, she'd take the key with her. She had the hostage now. Yeah, big talk! She started to cry for a second, then cut it off, cursing herself and breathing deeply. She looked down. Oh, God! Over two hundred feet to the sidewalk. She'd really build up some speed! She clenched her teeth and fought the terror, whispering, "You can do it. You can do it."

But even the gently gusting breeze was trying to pull her off.

Aziz and two of his men erupted out of the stairwell and split up to search. Aziz wandered toward the kangaroo crane. Where was she? . . . He glanced up and saw her thirty feet up on the other side of the gantry.

Dana froze in terror and locked her elbows around the cross-hatched steel, staring down at Aziz. Aziz raised his AK and fired a burst, trying to scare her, rounds clanging and ricocheting off the gantry just above her.

"Come down, now! Or I'll kill you!"

Dana wanted to say, "No you won't, 'cause I'll fall with the key!" But her throat wouldn't untighten. She hoped he wasn't stupid, unclamped her arms, and climbed higher.

Aziz cursed, slung his rifle over his shoulder, and started up after her.

Fast Faisil took his eye away from the camera eyepiece and looked around the room. One of the Crimson Creepos was staring up the stairwell toward the roof. The reporter interviewed a second toady six feet in front of him. The third guy, the only one with brains, was alert and on-station at the stairs to the twentieth, eyes checking the windows, the stairwell, the room, going back to the windows—

Faisil flipped open the secret compartment on his camera and pulled out a short-barrelled Walther. *Blam!* The hardcase by the stairs no longer had brains. Faisil spun 180 degrees: *Blam!* The guy at the roof stairwell took a bullet in his open mouth.

Another spin: *Blam!* Mr. Crimson TV Star fell on his back and slid across the floor, leaving a red skid mark.

The reporter stared at Faisil, for some reason (low self-esteem) expecting he was next. But Faisil only blew on the barrel of his gun and looked around with an I'm-so-bad look on his face.

"Jesus," said the newsman.

"Whoa," said Faisil, agreeing wholeheartedly. He brought up his rover.

"Fize here. I'm on the twenty-first. Twenty-first floor is secure. Approximately twelve faction members on the twentieth and no hostages. Repeat, no hostages on the twentieth, over."

Harry burned in low and fast from the Atlantic, screaming over eerily depopulated Miami Beach, over Biscayne Bay. He was seconds from the Madonna Building when he heard Faisil's update. Harry brought up his rover. "Faisil, where's Dana?"

"On the roof," came the reply.

But that wasn't strictly true. Dana was out on the crane's boom, moving horizontally out over the street. She was so terrified, she was almost in a trance.

Aziz crawled onto the boom behind her. The little bitch was driving him mad! She was as bad as her father! Well, he had sent *him* to Hell and he would send his whelp there; too.

Dana watched Aziz advance. He gained on her. She stopped for precious seconds and dug out the key. She dropped it out of her hand, letting it dangle at the end of the chain.

"No—!" yelled Aziz, reaching out. He almost shat his paratrooper pants.

"Don't come any closer! I'll drop it! I swear to God!"

Aziz raised his AK threateningly. "If you drop it, I will have no reason not to kill you." He kept coming calling her bluff. He had to overtake her before she got to the end of the boom. Once trapped, it would be clear to her she was dead whether she gave him the key or not. He would lose her then, and the key.

She backed away, slipped and lost her footing. "Oh!"

Aziz got another gray hair. "Easy, easy, child. Come on. Give me the key. Don't you want to live? I give you my word."

And then he smiled the fakest smile that Dana had ever seen. Dangling two hundred feet in the air, she still felt like laughing. It made her focus.

"No way, you whacko!" she said, and slid farther away.

Aziz went after her, moving quickly now.

Dana kept ahead. But things were getting even scarier. Out here at the end, the wind was making the boom sway back and forth. And worse than that, she had only a few yards left to retreat along.

The martyrs on the twentieth floor were on hair triggers. A small contingent prepared to storm up the stairwell to the twenty-first floor. They yelled to their comrades above.

"What's going on up there? What's all the shooting?"

An unfamiliar voice called down in fluent Arabic:

"Everything's fine. Don't bother yourselves. I've got it under control."

They looked at one another and muttered, "Who's that?" And then they heard a thundering. Then a screaming. Then a shrieking like they had never heard before. It seemed to come from above and below, from outside and inside. They looked in every direction—and then they saw.

The Harrier rose into view, hunchbacked and glowering disapprovingly, filling one whole window like a giant gargoyle from Hell. It was six feet away from the glass.

The terrorists jerked up their AKs just as Harry hit the trigger on his 25mm, six-barrel nose cannon. Depleted-uranium slugs, 6,000 rounds per minute. Harry swept the Harrier from one side of the floor to the other, pulverizing the glass, vaporizing the Crimson Jihad, mixing them both into a glittering red mist.

Aziz heard the rising shriek, too, and recognized it. He screamed to his men at the base of the crane: "Get the helicopter in the air! Go!"

And as Harry juiced the martyrs on the twentieth floor, the Aerospatiale pulled up and arced out over the city.

Aziz stayed on the boom. He swore to his God he was going to get the key and blow them all to Kingdom come.

Dana kept her eyes on Aziz, the chain dangling from her hand, sidling along the boom. She stepped out sideways and—whoa! She toppled, wrapping her arms around a metal stanchion. There was no boom left.

And Aziz crawled ever closer.

"Get away—!" she yelled, holding the key out over the street.

"I'll kill you!" bellowed Aziz.

A shrill roar suddenly flowered and enveloped them.

A satanic machine nosed around the side of the building like it was looking for something to kill.

Aziz cursed and froze. It was coming straight toward him. Then it dropped and slid directly under Dana. The canopy flipped back.

Aziz almost fainted. *"Renquiiiist!"*

"Dad!"

"Dana! Jump!" yelled Harry.

Aziz felt the migraine coming on again. Renquist was dead! Roasted like a pepper! Aziz had had enough! He brought up his sawed-off AK and sprayed one-handed.

The Harrier's back canopy shattered, and Harry ducked and spun the plane. The vertical stabilizer on his tail banged into the boom right next to Aziz, knocking him off balance.

Aziz grabbed for the boom with both hands, and his AK fell, bounced off the Harrier's tail and clattered down, catching on the intake scoop and hanging there.

But the same tail whack that startled Aziz, knocked Dana's feet off the boom. She hung from the last girder now, dangling over the street below.

"Daaaddyyy!"

Talk about bad timing. The Aerospatiale swung around the building at that very moment, and the Crimson door gunner let his M-60 go, ripping the nose and windshield of the Harrier, the line of bullets tracing up toward the cockpit.

Harry banked hard, taking the hits under the wing, slewing out of control as the copter pressed the attack.

Harry slid away fast, rounded a corner of the building, then spun 180 degrees and waited. The A-Star came around the corner in a big, sloppy turn, and found a Harrier looking right at it. The helicopter's pilot almost ripped his stick out of the floor trying to bank away as Harry's 25mm opened up and chased him. Harry let them go. Dana needed her daddy right now.

Dana screamed, her legs pinwheeling, looking around for Harry.

Aziz crawled toward her, eyes on the chain trapped in her hand, only a couple of feet away. He'd snatch the chain and make her fall all in the same motion. That would be fun!

But the Harrier was suddenly back, its nose hovering inches beneath Dana's feet.

"Let go, baby!" yelled Harry, unbuckling his webbing. "I've got you! Daddy's got you!" Harry reached for her, eyes flicking to his gas gauge. Hovering took two hundred pounds of fuel a minute. They didn't have much time.

Dana was scared. They hadn't covered jumping into Harriers in P.E. Class. Her face pleaded with her dad.

"Dad—!"

"Now, Dana!" he yelled.

She looked up. Aziz's hand was inches from her own. She screamed and let go, hit straddling the nose and slid backward as the jet bucked and tipped forward. Harry grabbed her forearm with his left hand, pulling her toward the shattered windshield, firing the puffers with his right.

"Grab hold, Dana!" he ordered her.

She grabbed the ragged edge of the shattered windshield.

"Ow! Dad, it hurts!"

"Hold on!"

Harry let her arm go. He needed two hands and two feet: He changed the nozzle vectors, worked the stick, and backed the Harrier away.

Aziz saw his grand plan, his life's work, the very meaning of his existence slipping away with the Harrier, leaving him tiny and all alone at the end of a boom in the middle of Miami. He had never felt tiny and meaningless before, and the shock hit him like a punch in the stomach. Every muscle in his body rebelled. He screamed and leapt out into space.

Aziz dropped twelve feet and landed astride the tail of the Harrier, still in the game.

The jet bucked and pitched. Dana screamed, her legs sliding backward and off the side of the nose. Harry reached for her with one hand, but couldn't help her. The plane was drifting out of control, rotating. Harry fought to stabilize it.

Aziz crawled forward, using his combat knife like a spike, stabbing the plane and pulling himself forward.

The ragged edge of the windshield sawed at Dana's fingers. She whimpered, then let go with one hand, pulled her jacket sleeve over her hand with her teeth, and grabbed the edge again. She did the same with the other hand.

Harry had the jet pretty stable again. He surged to

his feet, desperate to get Dana safe, grabbing both her forearms.

But you can't take both hands off a Harrier, ever. The plane spun and dipped wildly as Harry pulled Dana toward him, hooking her upper arms over the canopy edge. He sat back down and fought the spin. A flash in the corner of his eye—Aziz lunged from behind, knife arcing toward Harry's throat.

Harry blocked the blow upward, the blade slicing his forehead as he ducked away. He grabbed Aziz's wrist with one hand, and tried to control the Harrier's stick with the other.

Down below, where you'd normally see a crowd of ghoulish spectators, there were only military and law-enforcement people. And Gib—chewing his nonexistent nails. Gib watched the jet buck out of control, slide backward across the street and crash tail first into the Capitol Bank building, smashing out the windows of a conference room. He reached for his second pack of Rolaids.

The impact against the bank's windows dislodged Aziz and he lost his knife. He grabbed the conference room curtains to steady himself. The Harrier lurched forward again, and he tumbled into a backflip, landing nuts-first on the vertical stabilizer. Aaaaargh! He hugged the body of the plane with his arms and legs, grunting in agony. And then he saw his gift from Allah.

The sawed-off AK-47 dangled from its strap on the scoop right in front of him.

The plane crashed its way free of the bank building and plunged. But Harry battled his way back to a steady hover. He glanced over his shoulder and saw—

Aziz standing behind him, a short-barreled AK aimed not at his head, but at Dana's.

"Land the plane!" screamed Aziz. "Put the plane down on the roof or I kill the girl!"

Harry looked straight into Aziz's eyes and nodded assent. He turned to Dana, gave her a warning look, and flicked his eyes to the left. She tightened her grip and—

Harry banged the stick over, short but hard. The jet rolled and flipped Aziz off his feet. He slid down the wing, firing his AK wildly.

Aziz tumbled off the edge of the wing. The street came into view and his heart jumped into his mouth. He slid off, caught his breath to scream, then—

"Uhnn—!" Aziz found himself swinging underneath the wing's missile station. His battle harness had snagged on the fin of an AIM-9 Sidewinder.

Yes! God is Great! He brought up his AK and looked Harry in the eye.

Uh-oh, thought Harry.

Aziz squeezed the trigger. *Click.* The AK was empty.

Noooo! Would it never end?! He desperately tugged at the clip, pulling it out. A spare banana magazine was taped upside down to the first one. All he had to do was flip it over and shove it in.

Harry flicked his eyes over the ARBS weapons system display. Sidewinder . . . Sidewinder . . .

Aziz hoped Harry wasn't thinking what he thought Harry was thinking. He took his eyes off the gun to glance at the cockpit and fumbled the clip insertion. Shit!

Harry selected Sidewinder number three, and looked up. Through the blown-out twentieth-floor windows, he saw something that made him smile. The Aerospatiale slid by on the far side of the building, its open door bristling with Jihad warriors and M-60s.

Harry jinked the nose two feet, put his finger on the button, and looked at Aziz.

Aziz cocked the bolt on the AK and twisted around to shoot—

"You're fired," said Harry, and pushed the button.

The Sidewinder dropped and ignited, streaking away through the blown-out windows of the twentieth floor and out the other side into the A-Star.

Aziz threw his arms wide as he sped forward to embrace his comrades.

"Aaaaaaaaagh!" he said.

"Aaaaaaaaaaagh!" they said.

Kablooey. They fluttered down to the street in little meaty chunks mixed in their own flavorful juices.

"We're going down," said Harry, looking at his daughter. "You all right?!"

She nodded. She was all right.

Gib watched anxiously as the V.S.T.O.L. pitched and bucked its way down. The jet had been shot, stabbed, and beaten against buildings, and it was acting like the wounded beast that it was. He could see Dana hanging off the nose, sliding around as the plane fluttered toward the street.

A dozen Omega Sector agents formed the inner ring of dozens more federal agents clearing the area. No one without a top security clearance would get a look at the pilot of that plane or any member of his family.

Fifty feet more. The landing gear doors on the

Harrier broke open and the wheels deployed. Down it came, bouncing and bumping to a safe landing.

Harry stood up in the cockpit and grabbed his daughter's shoulders, pulling her into his arms, hugging her. Dana held him tight a moment, then looked at him. Her dad, an unbelievable badass dude, far cooler than any other dad on the planet.

"Hi, pumpkin," he said.

She grinned, wiped her eyes. "Do I look like a pumpkin?" she said.

He grinned back and lifted her over the side, putting her on the ladder. She climbed down into Gib's arms.

Gib keyed his rover. "Bring the limo up," he ordered.

An opaque-windowed limousine broke through the ring of Sector agents and drove up to the Harrier.

Its back door opened, and Gib shoved Dana into Helen's waiting arms. Harry leapt down from the Harrier and ducked in after them.

And they were whisked away.

A grateful, but virulently curious nation watched their televisions for weeks afterward, but only saw the same old aerial long shots of a girl and a big man ducking into a limousine. The pilot-hero was never identified, nor did anyone ever learn the part played by his daughter, the brave little thief.

But Dana did get to visit the White House and have dinner with the Pres. He was smart and funny. And with a greasy chili-fry hanging out of his mouth, he kind of reminded her of Gib.

Afterword

A year later, the Taskers were executing family dinners like a well-oiled machine. This October night, they were rounding out a delicious brisket dinner with slices of cheesecake and thumb wars.

"One two three four, I declare a thumb war," chanted Harry and Helen, fingers locked and thumbs ritually trading places on the "battle ground."

"Five six seven eight—Harry!"

Harry, as he had done all his life since he was five, cheated by jumping the gun.

"You lose!" he crowed.

"You cheated! Darn it, Harry! Start again!" yelled Helen.

Dana laughed. She knew what would happen next.

Helen began again, psyching herself for the struggle: "One two three four! I declare—! Harryyyy!"

Harry thought he was funny, pinning her thumb and not letting go.

"You're so easy!" he yelled.

Helen slapped at his arm. "Do it right!"

Harry cowered and mimed surprise: "You're such a sore loser!"

Dana laughed again, covering her mouth with her napkin before a chunk of potato could catapult out. She gulped some water, washing everything down. Enough chitchat. She stood up.

"I'm done," she said heading quickly for the door. Band practice wasn't for an hour, but she felt like she needed some peer pressure right away—

Harry caught her arm. "I seem to remember something about a history project due tomorrow."

Busted. "Dad," she said, "You just think you know everything." She trudged off to her room.

The phone rang. Helen went into the kitchen and picked up.

"Hello?"

"Boris and Doris?" said the voice on the other end.

"Go ahead," Helen said calmly, looking through the doorway and signaling to Harry. She listened for a moment then hung up.

"We're on," she said.

Black tie and tux. Harry looked sharp and badass. And Helen was the dish on his arm, elegant as a panther in a low-cut black gown and diamond choker. It was a reception on Embassy Row. A Central American nation honored its new Nobel Laureate, and everybody in Washington was there, inhaling culture, exhaling power.

Harry and Helen had never read a word by the author. They were there on Omega Sector business. The Central American country's Generalissimo For

Life (with a mustache) had arranged to import surplus Chinese tactical nukes in exchange for hard U.S. currency skimmed off his American aid. Trilby suspected the general would keep a handful of nukes, but broker the rest to other countries in exchange for mercenaries and oodles of conventional arms. The Hong Kong go-between for the deal was somewhere at the party. Sector was going to buy him out, or else start spanking people left and right.

Harry grabbed two flutes of champagne and handed one to Helen. They scanned the room.

Gib's subvocal voice came on in their ears: "So what's the scoop, team? You see your contact yet?"

Helen and Harry smiled and waved at the Dalai Lama and his agent. He gave them the sweetest smile they'd ever seen. The agent, that is. The Lama knew he had never seen these people before, in any lifetime.

Helen replied to Gib, speaking very low, "Not yet. But I see somebody else I've been wanting to see again for a *long* time."

Simon the Sleazebag, wearing a waiter's tux that was too small for him, grunted and pulled at the cork in a champagne bottle, speaking in a low voice to a young, Spanish-looking girl with an empty glass.

"This stakeout could get tricky," he muttered, eyes scanning the crowd. "You never know when things are gonna explode into a life-or-death situation. If things get rough, I'll contact you later. Maybe you should give me your phone number—"

Simon felt a vaguely familiar grip of steel take hold of his arm.

Harry pulled him up close and personal. "We meet again, Carlos," he said.

Simon dropped the bottle of champagne. It shattered on the marble floor.

Sharp fingernails dug into his other arm. He gasped and his head whipped around.

It was Helen, pressing something round and metal against the underside of his chin. Simon squealed like a distressed hamster.

"Honey," said Helen, "I'm just gonna do him right here."

"Go for it," said Harry enthusiastically.

"Oh, God," Simon groaned; and he peed himself noisily.

Helen whispered in his ear: "Fear is not an option."

Simon screamed and ran, falling over a tray of hors d'oeuvres, and tearing away toward the service doors.

Helen smiled like the cat that ate the canary, took the round, metal cap off her lipstick, and retouched her lips.

"Would you like to dance?" Harry inquired.

They dropped their flutes on a passing tray and swept off toward the dance floor.